ALL BECAUSE OF A BROKEN WATCH

AARINI ARZARE

For my little bro Adwin;

without whom, this book would never have come into existence.

Contents

Contents

I

I PICK UP SOME GARBAGE

All of this isn't going to make sense at first. But when you continue reading, you will understand what's going on. I don't know in which year. But you don't have much time left. It's going to come in the newspaper. It is going to come. It is coming, coming to end the human civilization. You are the only one who can save the future. Our future. Share this story with as many people as you can. We are dependent on you. Our future is dependent on you. And no, this is not about Global warming. It is about something bigger. Try to finish reading as soon as you can. Take out time and read this. You may not believe whatever I'm going to say. But if you want to save your loved ones' lives, read this, or you all are going to perish.

Hi, Aiden here. I am a sixteen-year-old boy, I usually don't like to describe myself but how else will you know how I look? (Just in case you meet me in the future.) So, here we go. I am a tall and muscular. I am very fair (I am not trying to make myself look good alright. So, don't judge me). I have brown, and long; silky straight hair that cover a bit of my eyes. I have had almond eyes which are sky-blue and I have long eyelashes. I have thin lips. My teeth are flashing white. I have short nails and have long and slim fingers. I have a dimple on my right cheek. I like to wear black leather boots whenever I go out. I am taller than most of my classmates (I don't know why i mentioned this). I like to play Minecraft and am flawless at it. My gaming skills are awesome. Don't get me wrong, I'm not praising myself.

Sorry, let's get back to where I stopped.

I have a stepbrother who is five years older than me. His name is Logan.

Logan is a short and plump guy (basically stout). He has bushy hair till his shoulder which covers his eyebrows. He is a fan of heavy metal and even has his own band. He is dark-skinned and always enjoys bullying me. He has siren eyes which are dark green and has short eyelashes. His teeth were yellow, and the teeth which were not yellow, were brown. He has long, dirty nails and short fingers.

From the start, our relation was not very good. Our mom, and our neigbours, were fed up of us. I remember several times when Logan heard his loud punk metal, the neighbours often came and complained, and my mom had to apoligise to them.

My stepmother used to care for Logan, but Logan was, my bad, *is* a moron and is too spoiled to help her out or even care for her. So eventually, I am the one who cares for my mother and am a bright child in school as well. Mother has put all her hopes on me and has long ago understood that Logan is good for nothing.

***

My mother was outside, shopping for groceries, while I was at home, doing my homework, and Logan, God knows where he was.

I was just about to start the last question when my phone rang.

I answered the call and said 'Yes Mom, any problems?'

'Hi Aiden, what are you doing?'- asked my tired mother.

'I was doing my homework Mom.'- I replied.

'Oh dear, I'm sorry, you can continue with your work, call me once you are done.'- she said quickly.

'No Mom, it's fine, you can tell me what you want.'- I said calmly.

'Oh, okay... uhm, actually I am feeling a bit dizzy. So, I will be going to the hospital, just to check if everything's fine. So, I will be getting a bit late.'- she said.

'Okay, I will take care of the house.'- I said softly.

'No, that's of no need.

I just want you to take out the garbage.'- said the mother.

That's all?'- I asked, surprised.

'Yeah honey, that's all.'- said mother.

Her voice was tired but calm. 'Okay Mum, I'll do it.'-I said.

Thank you dear.'- she said.

'Bye mum.'- I said.

With this, the phone hung up.

I decided to complete the last question and then take out the garbage.

As I had several things going on in my mind, there was no space for the little question to fit. Thus, I wasn't able to solve the question. So, I decided to take out the garbage first as an excuse to take a break and inhale some fresh air.

I headed downstairs, humming a song. I went into the kitchen, took out the garbage from the dustbin in our kitchen, and headed towards the backyard to put the garbage in the recyle bin. I made sure that the garbage bag was securely tied and put the garbage bag in the bin.

Once I was done with that, I wiped my hands with my jeans and started to head back to wash my hands. The moment I turned back, I bumped into something. Something tall. I looked up to find Logan standing in front of me.

'Sorry Logan.'- I said, trying to sound calm (which I was not) because I didn't feel like fighting with him. I knew that there was no point in arguing with him.

'Watch where you're going, idiot.'- said Logan and then sniggered.

With the urge to kill Logan straight away, I started to walk away from me with my hands in my pockets. That's when Logan pulled me back by the collar of my shirt and threw me towards the bin. I flew towards the bin and crashed into it, breaking the bin and tearing the dustbin bag, as a result of which, the garbage flew everywhere. My head had started to pain and I doubted that it may have started to bleed. I was starting to get up when Logan came up to me and said 'Take that, you nerd!'- and strolled away casually, as if nothing happened. I had no idea why he hit me after I said 'sorry'.

I sat up straight and pressed my finger to the back of my head. I winced a bit and I straightaway understood that there was a blood on the back of my head. When I brought my fingers in front of my eyes, I saw blood on my fingertips, as expected. Trying not to pay any attention to it, I got up and started cleaning.

Firstly, I had to clean up the mess and put it into a new dustbin bag as this one was torn apart. Secondly, I had to find a way to replace the broken bin and lastly, I had to do something about the wound on the back of my head, that too before my mum came.

I went inside the kitchen, took out the gloves, wore them, and went outside to collect the garbage in a new dustbin bag.

The garbage included two or three banana peels, some plastic bottles, some more plastic stuff, some seeds, leftover food, packaging materials, used tissue papers, organic materials... well, you get the idea.

And trust me, you don't want to smell it.

I started to pick up the garbage and put it into the dustbin bag. Every two minutes or so, I felt like puking. Once I was halfway there with cleaning up all the garbage, I spotted something shiny in it.

I lifted it, the light of that object was blinding me. I couldn't stand the light of the object. It was making my eyes burn. I felt as though I was being drawn towards it. I couldn't stand the urge to look at it, but it was as if the heat would burn my body.

Just then, a message popped up on my phone. I dropped the object and checked my phone. It was a message from my mother that said that she would be back in fifteen minutes.

This made me panic. I had to clean up the garbage but at the same time, I felt curious about that object as well, but there was no chance i could look at it in this light. So, I took the object in my hands slid it inside my pockets, and then quickly cleaned up the garbage.

My first mistake.

I put the dustbin bag aside and started to repair the bin with duct tape, as I couldn't find any other way to fix the bin.

Once I was done with that; somebody rang the bell, which I assumed to be my mum. Before going to open the door, I put the bag in the bin and went to open the door.

When I opened the door, the first thing I said was, 'What happened, is everything all right?'

'Yes Aiden, everything's fine. The doctor just prescribed me some medicines and said that I have a deficiency of Vitamin B12.' -said mum weakly.

'Oh, okay mum.'- I said; a bit worried, and gestured towards the grocery bag she was holding. She silently gave the grocery bag to me, and said Aiden, 'I am truly grateful to have a son like you.' With this, Mum started to walk towards her room to rest. I took out my gloves and threw them away.

I kept the bag in the kitchen and started to head upstairs to my room to complete my homework. Just then, Mom called out 'Hey Aiden, can you come down for a second.'

I silently came down, near my mother. 'Why is there blood on the back of your shirt?'- she asked sternly, despite her weak state.

I stammered, afraid to tell her the truth. I was scared that I would make Mum even more worried. 'I...uhm... uh... I...actually... I-I, while taking out the trash, I slipped and fell because of a banana peel.'- I ended, satisfied with my answer, praying that Mum would not catch my white lie.

'I am your mother; I can understand if you are lying.'- said Mum even more sternly.

I sighed. 'I put the trash in the bin and when I turned back, I bumped into Logan. I said sorry but then he pulled me back by the collar and threw me towards the bin.'- I said truthfully. Looking at my mother's worried expression, I said, 'It's fine. It's not hurting.'- I lied once more.

'I hope that you are not lying.'- said Mom after a pause. 'Of course, Mum, why would I lie to you.'- I lied innocently, although I felt bad after lying to Mum. I only lied to Mum as I didn't want her to worry about me (I am not a very big fan of lying, mind you).

'Mom, you need rest, allow me to guide you to your room.'-I said formally and guided her till we reached Mom's room.

After that, I ran upstairs to complete my homework, with the back of my head still bleeding a bit and paining a lot.

Once I was finally in my room, I sat down on my study table to do my homework. I was done with it in a minute or two. I then kept the notebook in my school bag and lay down on my bed to read a comic.

Okay, I agree it was dog man. I know it's a children's book, but I still like it. It was placed on the table, and I had no other book to read. Don't comment.

Anyways, time passed, the afternoon had arrived and lunch-time was near. The comic which I was reading was now finished.

It was a Friday and I was allowed to stay up till 11.

I was feeling bored. I then decided to read another book. When I had completed half the book, I heard Mum call out to me, 'Come down, lunch is ready.'

I rushed downstairs and sat on the table after washing my hands.

When I was done with my food, I ran upstairs to continue reading the book.

I had just finished my book and saw that it had only been an hour since I had eaten my lunch. The reading had taken up almost all of the energy in me, hence, I decided to sleep for a while.

The moment I kept the book on my study table and lay down on my bed, I fell asleep almost immediately.

☙

The next moment, I found myself being woken up by my mother. 'Aiden, wake up, dear.'- said mum softly.

I yawned, 'What time is it?'- I asked lazily.

'It's eight. It's dinnertime.'- said mum gently.

'IT'S EIGHT?!'- I exclaimed loudly. After hearing this, I was suddenly up and was brimming with energy.

I rushed downstairs to find that dinner was ready, waiting for me.

I served myself with some of my favorite salad and spaghetti. Once mom had joined me, I asked her, 'Where is Logan?'

'I asked him, but he said that he was having dinner at a friend's house.'- she said.

We had the rest of our dinner silently. I kept my plate near the sink once I was done with the food.

I then headed back to my bedroom, ready to play games until late noght. I took out my gaming computer, and gaming controller and started playing some random game (whose name I can't recall clearly).

I didn't realize the speed at which time flew by.

After what seemed like ten or fifteen minutes, Mum called out 'Aiden, it's time to sleep.'

'Yeah.'- I said obediently and closed my gaming computer, although I felt like playing more. Within five minutes, the lights of my room were switched off.

I wasn't feeling sleepy. I had been asleep for more than five hours in the afternoon.

My bed was right next to the window. The only thing that seemed to interest me was the closed shops glowing faintly in the pale light of the moon.

II

I REMEMBER THAT I HAD SOMETHING IN MY POCKET

That's when I remembered something. I laid straight on my back put my hand in the pocket of my jeans and took out the object that was reflecting blinding light in the afternoon sun.

I held it up in the pale glow of the moon. To my surprise, I saw that it was a golden watch. When I observed it a bit more closely, I realized that the belt of the watch was pure gold. *Who must have thrown it here, and why would they throw away such a valuable thing?* I wondered.

As far as I remembered, none of us had possessed a gold watch.

I then noticed that the time shown on the watch was wrong and the clock hands were not moving. I wore the watch and started to adjust the time using the crown. As I wasn't able to fix the time by holding the watch, I wore it and started to fix the time.

My second mistake.

The hands of the watch came to a stop at 11:50 and wouldn't just move ahead, no matter how hard I tried.

I thought that this might be the reason why the owner threw away the watch.

I tried to take out the watch from my hand. But it was as though it got locked on my hand. As though it was a part of my body. For a heartbeat, I thought that it would get stuck in my hand and would never come out. I thought that I would have to live with it for the rest of my life. I wanted to break it with a hammer but I had a feeling that it wouldn't come out even by using a hammer.

I closed my eyes and started to meditate. I realized that I was getting angry, frustrated, and annoyed. I then calmed myself down. I tried to make myself understand that anger and impatience only harm the individual practicing it.

But of course, it didn't work out. Why? Because I was no good at meditation and calming myself down, and I absolutely hate psychological stuff and motivational quotes because they make me feel even worse and depressed. They make you feel that you *are* depressed and need help (no offense to anyone. This is my point of view and I respect yours).

I was now really irritated by it. I tried to take the watch out, but it was really not of any use, to be honest.

After some five to ten minutes of trying extremely hard to take out the wristwatch, I had completely given up.

That's when I felt it. I felt as though I was being pulled inside the bed by hundreds and millions of hands around my body. I was finding it hard to breathe. I felt that my whole body was being compressed. I felt as though the pressure would crash my ribs into atoms. I didn't know what to do. The feeling was unbearable, and it felt as though it was going on forever, it was suffocating me to death. I felt that this was the end of me. I wasn't able to think. The pressure had squeezed out the ability to think from me.

The next moment, I felt like I was falling into nothingness, the compressing feeling had now gone. I was falling into complete darkness. There was no sound at all. I couldn't even hear myself scream my lungs out. I felt as though somebody had extracted my voice box from me.

For a moment, I felt that I was Aiden in the wonderland, except that there were objects falling down with Alice, but in this case, there was complete darkness and silence.

I tried to look for a way to exit that place. I had started to panic. I couldn't understand what to do. I was freaking out completely. I could feel myself sweating with fear. When I looked at my bare hands, I saw that my hands were white. When i looked at my clothes, they were in black and white, but I remembered that I was wearing blue jeans and a coloured t-shirt.

I tried to calm myself down, trying to force my brain and heart into believing that it was just a nightmare, nothing else (although I had a feeling that this was not a nightmare), and in a minute or so my mother would be waking me up... or maybe not.

I then saw light ahead, and I noticed that I was falling towards it. In a heartbeat, I was down, lying straight on my back with several people chatting around me, walking past me, as though they didn't see me. The place looked as if it was a busy street in New York. But I was sure that it was not New York.

I stood on my legs; which were still wobbly. My legs felt like water. I had a feeling that if I moved my legs even by a millimeter, they would collapse. In fact, my whole body felt that way. My whole body had gone numb. I felt as though even if a wasp or bee stung me, I would feel nothing.

I realized that I was standing in the middle of the road. But I was in no fit condition to move. I closed my eyes and moved my leg. After a few seconds, nothing happened. I opened my eyes, I was alright. I then casually started to walk on the pedestrian walkway. When I was almost there, I spotted a shop that was labelled as 'The LEGO Store'.

I couldn't contain myself. Although I had no money with me; I just wanted to take a peek inside the store.

I looked behind me to spot a zebra crossing, ignoring the fact that it was not there before. I was so sure about it because I had just walked on that path.

Before walking on that zebra crossing, I looked up, expecting to find a random black hole in the sky (it was from where I had fallen).

As expected, I didn't find any random black hole popping in the middle of the sky. I was now completely convinced that this was a dream and all of this was my imagination, I started to believe that it was all well and Mom was going to wake me up any moment now. In a blink, I was walking on the zebra crossing, my hands in the jean's pockets, whistling the song 'dance of death' (for thos I was in a very good mood. I was doing a countdown in my mind in which I would wake up. But as always, I had spoken too soon.

Hey, did I tell you that during a test, I had said that the questions were too easy and the moment I said that, the next set of questions were eating everyone's brains. And did you know that one time I- Sorry, yeah, back to the story.

Just then, a car came at full speed towards me. I put my hands over my face and was ready to die.

When nothing happened, I saw that a sinkhole had appeared out of nowhere, which must have prevented me from dying. Out of curiosity, as I stepped closer to the sinkhole to check how deep it was, I bent a little, maintaining my balance. That is when I felt as though somebody pushed me from the back and I fell inside the sinkhole.

I had the same feeling of falling into nothingness, all because of the watch. I now regretted wearing it.

I was still falling, and this time, I was not at all surprised that the darkness seemed unending.

I was kind of happy that I didn't have nyctophobia (the fear of darkness) and scopophobia (the fear of being watched). After a minute or so, I spotted light. I started to swim in the air, trying to reach the light faster.

I then fell onto the ground, and this time, it hurt. I hit my head on the ground really badly. My vision had started to get fuzzy. I tried to stay from fainting, but my head burnt very much. (IT WAS THE SAME PLACE WHERE I HIT MY HEAD ON THE BIN!). I felt that it was the end of me. The wound was throbbing with pain. I felt that I would keep on sleeping and never wake up.

(But unfortunately, I did, and that is why the story keeps going on)

III

I AM AN ANT

I didn't know for how long I had been asleep. But that thought didn't bother me. I now understood that this was no dream. I understood that this was no video game. I understood that I had to escape this, as fast as possible. I had to find the exit... only if there was one.

The watch had reappeared on my hand. I tried removing it, but no luck. I understood that it was the watch that did this to me. If I could just get rid of that.

Now that I had woken up, I started to look around for doors or anything that may be related to an escape.

But unfortunately, I could not find a door. I had now understood that this was no nightmare, nor it was my imagination.

I had an idea about what could have happened ... that could not have been possible, humans had not discovered how to do that yet.

I put aside that thought and looked around, to get an idea of that place.

When I looked around, I felt like an ant, standing in front of a human. The buildings around me were massive. The smallest building I could see was about the size of Burj Khalifa. The width of the building could fit about three hundred to five hundred elephants comfortably.

I didn't feel like any of these buildings were in any country I knew. Some of the buildings were levitating in mid-air. The doubt in my mind had been cleared. This could not be reality, just my imagination. Dude, I mean what kind of building levitates in mid-air?!

I looked behind and my eyes fell on a building that was so tall that I couldn't see where it ended.

I started to explore around the buildings, still trying to find some exit, although I had a feeling that there was none.

I turned back to explore some other building, and that's when something hit me on my head and landed in front of me.

I took a step back cautiously, wondering if that thing would attack me once again. When nothing happened for a while, I came closer to that thing to take a closer look at it.

It looked like metal. It was really small. I went closer to it and picked it up.

I started to examine the metal piece, trying to figure out what that tiny particle might belong to.

While examining the tiny metal piece, another metal piece fell in front of me. Except that this one was a bit bigger than the first one.

I kept the metal piece I was examining down and picked up that thing that had just fallen in front of me. When I picked it up, I realized that it weighed much more than the first one. I tried to join together the two pieces, trying to make sense of it. I don't know why but I tried to make out the connection between them. I thought that it was a part of something bigger. I thought that I was trapped in an escape room and this was a part of the puzzle which I needed to solve in order to escape.

After observing it for a while, it did look like they were a part of something really big. I didn't know how I knew it; I just knew it. It looked as if it was torn apart by hand. I didn't know how someone could tear apart metal by bare hands. I could figure out that this was one of the smallest parts of the unknown thing.

But who would tear them apart like this? I wondered.

As I delved deeper into the details and the edges of that piece of metal and squinted my eyes, I saw that the metal pieces were made with really fine details, and I was sure that no human could have made this (and I was right, no human made it. Oh Sorry, no spoilers).

While I was examining the pieces, once again another piece came crashing in. I was startled for a moment but then I had the feeling that I had to solve this puzzle destiny had given me. I felt that this could be the way in which I could go back home. Without wasting any more time, I ran towards the piece that had just fallen.

I had to solve this jigsaw puzzle to get home (at least that was what I thought at that point in time).

Although I knew that if this was not the right thing and the right time to do it, I would have no other opportunity to go home.

This thought didn't bother me as I had a feeling that I was doing the right thing.

I picked up the piece. That one was as heavy as the previous one. I noticed that the detailing was very fine in this one as well.

When I started to examine the pieces, I realized that this piece was somehow connected to the second piece, but not directly, there was one more between them. I felt stupid at that point. I mean, how could I figure out that two of the pieces were connected but there was another piece between them? I mean, HOW?

While I was figuring this out, I was expecting another piece to come flying and fall in front of me. Unfortunately, that didn't happen.

After some ten minutes, I was now tired of waiting for another piece to come and fall, so I assumed that I had to go look for another one.

I turned around to face the direction from which the broken metal pieces had come. I started to walk toward the direction where the pieces had come flying from. That's when I spotted something shining in the departing rays of the setting sun from the corner of my eye.

I turned back and saw that there was a tiny rectangular object, just a few feet away from me. I took it in my hands when I reached it. I saw that it was really tiny, tinier than the 'ESC' button on a computer.

It took me a moment to realize what it was. It resembled a computer chip. Although it was not exactly like the one I had seen before, it was similar.

Without wasting any more time on the chip, I proceeded toward the direction where I had seen the metal coming from. I knew it was a bit dangerous, but anyway went towards it. I was not sure what I would find on that side. The view from the other side was obstructed by a large building.

Cautiously, but excitedly, I walked towards the building. Once I had reached the building, I inhaled deeply, closed my eyes as I took a deep breaath, and peeped from behind the window.

What I saw, left me speechless for a minute or two, and then I experienced fear, then excitement, and after that astonishment. I was experiencing a lot of feelings together, so it was hard to decide which feelings not to give importance to and which ones should I prioritize.

IV
I WANT TO DIE

At first, I thought I was daydreaming. I thought that the tiredness and the stress had drained me out. But everything seemed so realistic. I would figure out if I was trapped in a game like it happened in most of the fictional movies I had seen.

After some ten minutes, I forced myself to believe that I was not imagining things, whatever I saw was happening in real life. I could feel it, I could feel the ground shaking. I could see it; I could hear it.

What I saw was very surprising indeed. I could not speak, my mind wasn't functioning, and I wasn't able to process the information, the events, the things that were happening around me. I don't know how I can explain it to you. You can't even visualize what I saw. Anyway, let me try to tell you what I saw.

I was currently seeing some 20-meter-tall transformers.

The next creature I saw was the main reason why I had so many feelings at once.

I saw huge aliens. They were giant apes. And by giant, I mean literal giants. So, they've got thick fur all over their body. They've got big, sharp claws and their furious yet calm eyes covered with their thick bushy eyebrows. When they roar out in anger, it's like thunder booming all around, showing who's the boss in the unknown world.

Their head is protected by a helmet made of metal. Their upper body was covered with metal armor and their boots were made up of the same. Their armor looked like they were unbreakable. Their nails were the size of a full-grown horse. Altogether, they were a bit bigger than the blue whale.

It looked as if there was a war raging between both of them. Both sides were fighting pretty aggressively.

When I looked a bit closely, I saw that several apes were battle-scarred, some of their wounds looked freshly cut.

I was so immersed in watching them fight that I completely forgot about the metal pieces that I had wanted to find.

I peeped more from behind the window to see clearly. A bunch of apes then ran towards the giant transformers-like-robots, and I had to hold the building so that I won't fall down.

I then moved a bit more towards the front.

Then suddenly an idea struck my mind. I had this weird feeling. I felt really excited about the war going on. As the creatures were so humongous, I could barely see their head, so, to get a better view, I wanted to get to the top of the building. Although I knew that it was a really stupid, and silly idea, I did it.

I inspected the building up and down, and spotted an entrance to the building. But there was a problem, the entrance was all way to the other side. It was on the place where the battle was raging.

I had to get to that door, somehow. But I didn't figure the 'somehow' yet.

Although I knew it was really stupid of me to do it. It could risk my life. I still did it. I was way too excited to be bothered by this thought.

I started to walk towards the door, keeping in mind to maintain distance from the giant apes and robots, in fear of getting squashed like a bee.

I was keeping my back glued to the building while walking. I then saw a robot head cut off from its body, and what's worse is that it was coming at me with full speed. I ducked and covered my face with my hands.

After a moment or two, I was ready to open my eyes and find myself in heaven. But luckily when I opened my eyes, I found myself in the same place, battle raging, robots being torn apart, and the thunderous roar of the giants. I then looked at the building and saw a big dent on the building. When I looked down at my feet, I saw the robot head.

With my heart pounding, I wondered what would have happened to me if he hadn't seen the robot head.

Without thinking what I was doing, I took a step forward and kicked the head like a football with all my might.

My third mistake.

When the robot head went flying and hit an angry looking battle-scarred ape, I realized what I had just done. The battle-scarred ape looked at me with angry eyes which were partly hidden by his thick and bushy eyebrows. My stomach did a back flip, and I had a feeling that this could be the end of me.

The scarred ape roared with anger at me. Some drops of the saliva of the ape fell on me, and I could smell the ape's bad breath.

The thing which I had feared had now happened. I hadn't wanted to divert the attention of the apes and the robots. Unfortunately, that is what happened.

The ape roared with rage once more and advanced towards me.

I ran as fast as I could and entered the building. I saw around me and saw a humongous and beautiful room. The floor was once made with white marble, which was now broken and dirty because of the war. I saw a glass chandelier hanging from the ceiling. The chandelier was enormous, it was almost ten times the size of a normal chandelier.

The room was like a five-star hotel lobby, but way bigger. I was dazzled by the beauty of the room. I felt as though I could live his whole life there, in the beautiful lobby. I wondered whether it was a hotel, or was it a-

Then I heard the angry roar of the ape, I was then pulled back into his senses, I then realized that I had a giant ape chasing me and may kill me. That ape could smash me with his legs or squeeze me in his fists.

The thought of this made me shudder from head to toe. I wanted to call the lift, but there was none. Even if there was, I couldn't spot it at that point in time.

I looked around and saw steps leading upwards. I ran towards the stairs.

I was on the footstep of the stairs when I realized that there was a major problem. I was like a miniature in this world, so everything around me was triple my size, and so were the stairs. The first step was almost till my waist. I didn't have time to find another way to escape the giant. Even if I had some other way to escape the giant, I couldn't think of any.

Without wasting another second, I started to run up the stairs as fast as I could. I couldn't skip a step as I used to do at home, as the steps were way too big for my little, tiny legs to skip them.

When I had crossed some five or six floors, I started to sweat and my speed decreased. After three more floors, I believed that I had lost the ape. I was sure that ape was not that tall that I could reach the ninth floor. I sat down with my back sticking to the first step which leaded to the eighth floor. I relaxed for a while.

I inhaled, and then exhaled, inhaled, and then exhaled. I took a few dep breaths to stabilize I breathing and I heartbeat. My heart was beating really fast, I felt as though if I didn't rest and stabilize my heartbeat, my heart would leap right out of my chest and jump away, and I could do nothing other than to sit and watch the heart jump away.

I was relieved that I could outrun the ape. I smiled at myself while breathing deeply. I wanted to go back down and find myself some shelter or some safe place where I could rest for a while and stay safe from the apes.

I could see three options in front of me. Option one, I could go down and search for a shelter; option two, I could go to the top and view the fight, and the rest, I would decide later; option three, I could stay in this hotel, or house or villa, or whatever, and it would fulfill any of my needs.

'But,'- I thought to myself. 'There may be some exceptions. I can't take any risk going down again as there may be a shrewdness of apes waiting for me down there. I can't go up on the top as well, because the angry looking ape might be waiting for me down there. I guess option three sounds the best.

I closed my eyes and imagined myself gazing outside a big glass window which replaced the wall of one side of the room. It had a beautiful, crystal white study table on my left side. My luxurious and comfy bed. And here I was, in my white bathrobe, holding a warm cappuccino in my hands. The feeling of satisfaction and peace overwhelming me.

And here was, lying on the floor like a complete hobo.

I smiled at myself. I couldn't wait to make this dream of mine come true. I advanced towards the rooms of the seventh floor. As expected, the rooms and the doors were huge. The corridors seemed unending. I couldn't see where the rooms where ending.

I looked around to find any open rooms by chance. To my surprise, I found an open door just a few rooms away. I couldn't believe my stroke of luck. 'I guess it's my lucky day.'- I muttered to myself happily and started to walk towards the room, singing songs to myself with hands in my pockets.

Once I had reached the door of the room, I took a little peep inside to check if anyone one was inside. This room as well was empty. At this point I couldn't believe how lucky this day was getting.

I whistled happily and entered the room.

First of all, I wanted to take a quick shower. But unfortunately, I realized that this building was made by the robots, and they did not need a bath. Disappointed by this, I now wanted some good sleep. Once again disappointed, I realized that robots needed no sleep.

Now frustrated by anger and disappointment, I stamped my foot on the ground that I (don't know how) twisted my ankle.

Even more irritated and annoyed, I sat down on the ground and tried to calm myself down through meditation.

As you know, I really bad at meditating and calming myself down.

That's when I heard another thundering roar. I opened my eyes and turned my head to look outside the window.

At least the window replaced the wall on one side of the room. I was happy about that. But, the scene outside the window was terrifying.

V

I ALMOST DIE

The moment I saw what it was, my heart beat increased, I started to panic. My brain was not functioning properly.

What I saw was not a big deal, but if you were in my place, I bet you would react no differently.

I saw the great battle-scarred ape once again, and the ape was way angrier than before. I had now understood that if I did not run for my life now, then it was the end of me. Before running away, I decided that I could apologize to the ape before running away and making the ape even angrier. I knew that this was a really stupid idea, and if the ape did not agree, it would be worse. I knew I could die if the ape misunderstood him, but it was worth a try.

I stood as calmly as I could. There was sweat glistening on my face. I wanted to look calm, but deep down I knew that I was looking scared, and not at all 'calm'.

I was facing the window. I was trying to calm myself down, I took deep breathes, but none of this worked. It's hard to keep calm when there's such a big, muscular and scary looking ape right in front of you. It's hard to keep calm when you have absolutely no plan, and you don't know what will happen to you the very next second. It's hard to keep your calm when you are precariously balancing on the tip of death. It's hard to keep your calm when it's a matter of your life, and you are merely depending on a fluke, or just playing luck.

There were thousands of thoughts going on my mind. Like- What would happen if I couldn't escape? What if I couldn't convince the ape? The giant already looked so angry, what if he misunderstood what I wanted to express? What if he understood and let me go? What would happen after that? Will the ape complain about me to the king and the whole army of the apes come to kill me? That won't be possible as the whole army would be busy fighting with the robots. But what if-

That's when the battle-scarred ape hit the glass window with such a force that it shattered into pieces. Ripping my jeans, the glass pieces pierced through my skin. My right leg had several big pieces of glass stuck to it. My arms had glass pieces stuck as well. I had been thankful that none of the glass had hit his face.

Despite the pain in my leg and hands, I still stood as bravely as I could.

My leg had started to burn. I was sure that the wound had already started to bleed.

I was about to apologize, but then I realized that I didn't know how I would apologize.

The battle- scarred ape gave a thunderous roar. The roar boomed across the room, making it sound even louder. I did not take much time to realize that there was no peace he could make with this ape and realized that the only way I could escape from this giant was to run away.

I ran towards the door. I opened it and started to limp towards the stairs. I was about to climb the stairs when I saw the lift. I wanted to go through the lift, but I didn't know how I was going to reach it. At this point, I didn't even know where the lift was. I was begging to God to save my life.

When I was sure that this was the end of me. I decided that I might have one percent chance of surviving if I took the stairs.

I had just crossed one step, when my leg started to hurt so much that I fell from the stairs. And when I fell, I fell on my right leg and I felt the glass pierce even deeper into my skin.

I screamed in agony. But my scream was muted by the booming roar of the scarred ape.

I then heard another voice; it was neither mine nor the apes. Still lying on the floor, I looked front and saw that the voice coming was from the wall.

After a few seconds, I realized that it was coming from the lift. I was so thankful that God had listened me.

The doors of the elevator were opening. I tried to get up, but I couldn't. I couldn't feel his right leg. I felt that it had been chopped of my body and thrown away.

I started to crawl towards the lift as fast as I could. Only with my left leg and arms, I merely dragged his right leg.

With another thunderous roar, I realized that the ape was getting closer.

Luckily, I was able to enter the lift right before it closed. I then saw that there were several buttons on the lift. I had started to panic once again. I didn't know what to do. I tried to press the top button but I was too short to do it. So, I pressed the lowest button after jumping as high as I could (Sorry, I couldn't jump. I went on my toes and stretched my arms to their fullest).

I had expected to go down. At this point, I didn't care whether I went up or went down, I just wanted to escape from the ape. Luckily, the lift started to move upwards with speed.

I leaned back and sighed in relief. I smiled to myself. 'That was easy.'-I laughed to myself.

Once again, I had spoken too soon.

I then started to notice everything around me. That's when panic and fear started to grip me. First of all, it was a capsule; second, it was a glass lift. It was transparent and it would give away my location

I wondered how long it would be before the ape realized where I was. I looked down and saw that the coast was clear, and I was very well above the ground. I sighed and wished that I would reach the top before the ape could see me.

I kept glancing down. I knew that the speed of the lift wouldn't increase even if the ape was nearby.

I relaxed my shoulders as I thought that the ape won't be able to come till this height. I knew that the ape couldn't fly or jump till here.

I looked around to enjoy the view. But the moment I looked sideways towards my right, I saw that the ape was climbing the building and was just a few meters below me. I wanted to scream with fear, but I knew I would give away my place.

It won't be long before the giant had spotted me. I crossed my fingers and hoped that the giant won't spot me.

The lift was advancing at quite a speed I must say, but not at the speed that it could outrun the ape.

Today was my unlucky day. The ape had spotted me and was climbing at his full speed. 'Come on dude, you've got to be kidding me.'- I said to myself.

The ape was climbing at the same speed as the lift. I had now freaked out. I only had a few seconds in hand before the ape smashed the lift and I would fall down.

There was a battle raging below me, and I was quite sure that if I fell down, I would be trampled below the legs of the apes or the robots.

I had to think fast or-

The ape was now coming closer and closer. I was panicking. My mind went blank. I could never think in stress. I didn't want to die so early. I wanted to see my mum before I died. I closed my eyes and was ready to die.

The ape smashed the lift and I opened my eyes. I got hold of the ape's hair on the back. When I looked down, I saw that the glass pieces had fallen down completely and the lift had exploded.

I would not have any chances of survival if I hadn't gotten hold of the hair on the back of the ape. The scarred ape was still climbing upwards.

He had not realized that I was hanging on his back. I wondered where the ape was heading. I did not dare make a move in fear that

the ape would realize that there was someone on his back. I held on as tight as I could. My hand had also started to bleed because of the glass stuck to it.

Despite the pain in my hand, I hung on tightly. In some time, me and the ape reached the top.

I was just about to get down when the ape's hand reached me, the ape picked me up with his hands and raised me up right n front of his face.

He threw me on the ground with such a force that I hit my head on the ground and it started to bleed.

The glass in my skin pierced even more deeper into my skin. There was a river of blood which was flowing from my head. My whole shirt was drenched in blood. I had realized that I had already lost a lot of blood.

I tried to look up at the ape, but my vision had gone fuzzy. I didn't have the strength to even stand up. My whole body had been aching. The glass had already given me so much pain. My whole body had now gone numb.

I let my head rest on the floor. Before closing my eyes, I heard another booming roar and knew that it was the end of me. I realized that the ape had known all along that I had been on his back. The ape had been waiting for the correct moment to strike.

How could he not have noticed a puny little human hanging on his back?

With this, I closed my eyes...

VI

I BECOME ALIVE AFTER DYING (and I'm not a ghost)

When I woke up, I didn't know for how long I had been lying unconscious. I had been thankful that I hadn't lost my life.

Moral of the story: never do anything stupid which may risk your life. Even if there is less than one percent chance that it may risk your life, don't do it because it *will* risk your life.

I was covered in blood. I was pretty sure that I had lost over a liter of blood.

After regaining conscious, I lay there on the ground still, as still as a doll. The blood coming from the wound in my head had dried up, and so did the wound on my arms and legs.

I sat up straight, with my hands preventing me from falling back down. I looked on the floor to see a lot of dried blood on the ground, which I assumed to be the blood which had oozed out of my head.

I tried to stand up, but I was too weak to even stand. My vision was now much clearer than before. I didn't know how I survived after losing so much blood. Usually, a person can die if they lose two to four liters of blood.

I still couldn't feel my legs, nor I was able to move them. I crawled backwards and rest my back on the railing of the building.

I brought my hands in front of my eyes and looked down at the shattered pieces of glass stuck to it. I knew it was going to pain a lot but that was the only I could avoid having any infection.

There were two glass pieces stuck to my right arm. One piece on my forearm; and one on my shoulder.

I took a deep breath before pulling out the pierced glass from my skin. I screamed with agony. More blood started to come out of the wound. It looked as if somebody had just painted half of my hand with blood-red colour (No, I mean seriously, it looked like fake blood).

The wound had started to hurt even more after I had pulled the glass piece out. For a moment, I wished that I hadn't pulled that out.

After gathering all of my courage, I pulled out the other glass piece stuck to my shoulder.

I shut my eyes and tears flowed silently out of it, and I let them flow. The dry, salty tears flowed down through my eyes, and then it dropped down to the floor.

With another scream of agony, I pulled out the glass on my left arm. This time, I was sure that my scream would not be muted by another booming roar of some giant.

Tears still dripping from my face, I just touched the glass stuck to my legs and winced in pain. The piece was buried deep inside my flesh. I had a feeling that I would have to cut open a bit of my flesh to take out the glass.

I somehow managed to take the glass out of my leg without tearing my flesh open (I would be pleased to describe the feeling to you but it was really very painful and disgusting). I did scream on the insides but not on the outside, as I didn't dare drag any apes near me. Especially not that one. With that, I wondered why the ape didn't kill me. Well, I must agree that I was thankful for that.

The next task was to find some water to drink and to clean my wounds. Firstly, I had to cover up my wounds from something to stop it from bleeding.

I looked around but I couldn't see anything to cover my wounds except for one.

I tore out a bit of my shirt and wrapped it around the wound on my right leg. After tearing one more part of my shirt and covering the wound on my left leg, I started to limp towards the door which was present at the far end of the rooftop.

I didn't cover the wounds on my arms as I felt they were not as deep as the ones on my legs, and I didn't want to tear more of my shirt as the sun was setting and I had a feeling that things were about to get cold.

I opened the door and saw the lift. I was about to call it when he realized something. When the ape was chasing me in the lift, I pressed the lowest button to go up (after jumping as high as I could). So, I had to press the highest button in order to go down.

And at this point I was so pissed off at my day that I felt like going back on the rooftop and jumping from God knows how many floors, maybe hundred?

I then decided to take the stairs as I was in no fit condition to jump and run. I was not even in a condition where I could walk normally, but what else could I do?

With difficulty, I reached the ground floor in a few hours.

Before stepping outside, I looked around the magnificent and enormous lobby, my eyes searching for a sip of water they could not find.

Even more disappointed and frustrated by my luck, I decided to go outside in search of water and food. Before going outside, I looked around to see that no one was around. There were no apes nor were the robots around.

Not letting this opportunity slip from my hands, I sneaked out of the hotel lobby into the cold and chilly atmosphere of the deserted battleground. Which I knew was not deserted long ago.

I was sure that it was a battleground as there was some fresh blood, as well the blood that stained the ground. There were several massive weapons lying on the ground.

When I looked closely, I saw that the weapons were made up of wood. I wondered how the apes could have slayed and broken the metal robots with wood.

For a split second, I forgot all about my desperate thirst of water, my hunger for food, and need for shelter.

A chill wind whispered through my ears which made me shiver. I kept my hands in my jean's pocket to keep them warm.

I started limping towards the opposite side of the building, shivering slightly. I knew that the robots needed no protection from wind, rain or fire, but the apes did.

I was still a bit scared after what had happened to me. I was afraid that I might meet the scarred ape again, and if that happened, I won't be able to survive it.

After a few minutes of walking, the wind started to blow, making it even colder.

The jeans were not at all helping me to stay warm. I started to jump around and do some exercises in order to keep my body warm. I didn't want to focus on the cold.

My mom used to say that feeling cold or hot is just a game of the mind. *If you convince your mind that it is cold, then it is extremely cold. If you convince your mind that you need a warm blanket to protect you, you will feel even colder. The same thing goes for warm temperatures. In cold temperatures, if you divert your attention to the surroundings and force your mind into believing that you are feeling warm and not cold, it will make you feel warmer. I cannot guarantee that you will not feel cold, but you will feel better.* said the soft voice of mum in my mind.

I had never tried this out, I was going to try this technique now. I started to divert my attention to the buildings and the setting sun. I diverted my attention to the things around me and repeatedly told my mind that I was feeling warm and not cold.

My gaze was fixed upon the departing rays of the sun. While staring at the pale-yellow rays, I wondered what my mother was doing. For the first time, I thought about Logan.

While thinking this, my throat suddenly felt dry and my stomach made a low growling sound that made me even more thirsty and hungry.

After a minute or two of staring at the departing rays of the sun, I bumped into something.

I looked ahead and saw a forest of redwood trees. As far as I knew, there were the tallest trees on earth and only 80,000 were remaining in California.

I couldn't help myself from saying 'wow' at this. I had always wanted to see Redwood trees. They were on my bucket list. I felt that I could climb up the tree and live the rest of my life on one of the branches, if I hadn't wounded my leg so badly.

Seeing the redwood trees, I realized that I was now in the area of the apes.

I looked around and saw that the trees seemed to keep on going. The seemed unending. But there's an end to everything in this world.

I looked around for any pathway or any markings which would lead me to a well of water or a bit of food.

And I saw a path which led deep into the forest. Since I had no torch or flashlight, I wanted to reach to the end of this before it became dark.

I knew that this could be a trap for the robots, if they wanted to infiltrate the apes' territory without them knowing. But after a few minutes of investigating, I saw footsteps on the path. So, I decided that this was the path to water, food and shelter (and apes).

The rays of the sun had departed and the sun had hidden behind the mountains. Without wasting any time, I started to limp as fast as I could.

Although I didn't have nyctophobia, I was still afraid of the animals present in the forest.

It was pitch black after a few minutes I was into the forest. I was feeling even more thirsty, and as it was so dark, I didn't even know how close or far I was from all the things that I needed to live.

Presently, I was sure that I would either die out of cold, or would die out of thirst and hunger, or both of them.

At this point, I could eat anything that I would get.

Limping had made my leg hurt even more, and for a moment I had a feeling that someone was following me. But I did not dare look back.

I couldn't see anything as it was so dark. I barely even knew where I was doing.

Luckily, I spotted light coming from a distance. A warm feeling of hope spread over me. For a moment, I had a feeling of happiness. For a moment, I forgot all about my pain and misery. I wanted to fly towards the light, I wanted to run. But I had to limp.

In a few minutes' time, I reached the light.

I covered my eyes, as the light could have blinded me. When I opened my eyes, I saw that it was dark once again.

I assumed that it would be the apes' sleeping time.

Just a few minutes ago, the sun had set. I was sure that it was not even 8:30. I wondered why the apes slept do early. Then I realized that the gorillas and the apes sleep for up to twelve hours a day, or sometimes seventeen as well.

I heard several noises coming from the village; which I assumed to be snoring noises.

Quietly, I started to walk towards the place where the apes were sleeping.

While I was walking, I felt that my shoe suddenly felt a little wet.

I felt ecstatic as I touched the ground to feel wet mud. I moved my fingers even further on the ground to feel a pond of water.

I cupped my hands together and started drinking water from it. I never felt more happier to drink water. I had never valued water before. But today, I had realized that there was no juice, soda, or shake that could meet the requirement of water.

Soon after drinking water, I limped backwards towards the place where the redwood trees were planted. I decided to sleep under the tree for the night.

The moment I lay flat on my back, I felt the soft grass on my back, which was surprisingly not pricking me. I curled myself up, about to sleep. Just then, I realized something. I remembered that trees produce a small amount of carbon dioxide in the night and that I am most probably going to find it hard to breathe when both the organisms are producing only carbon dioxide.

I got up from there and limped towards the village. For the rest of the night, I slept facing the village. Exposing only a bit of my head and legs to the village.

The moment my head touched the ground, my eyelids felt heavy with exhaustion of the day. I almost immediately closed my eyes and drifted to the world of dreams...

VII
MEETING COCO

When I opened my eyes, I didn't even realize the fact that I was lying on a hammock which was made up of branches and was hundred times bigger than a regular one. I turned my face to the sky to see sunlight piercing through the leaves. I felt the warmth of the morning sun on my body. Honestly, that was one of the the best feelings I had in this world.

I yawned and stretched myself. For a minute, I stared at the leaves of the trees.

I sensed something was not right. I looked a bit closely to see that the leaves were not of redwood. They were of the Uganda Ironwood tree.

The moment that name popped up in my mind, I realized what was going on, or at least made an assumption of what was going on.

The Uganda ironwood trees are the trees on which apes sleep. I remembered that apes slept in temporary bed or platforms. They bend or break the branches to create a bowl-like shape which they usually line with leafy twigs.

I had now understood that I was lying on a bowl-like hammock made up of branches and twigs about five-hundred to seven-hundred meters above ground.

I had to get out of there before any of the apes spotted me. I turned my head towards my right to find some way to escape from here. That's when I thought that I saw an ape swing on one of the branches from the corner of my eye.

When I looked towards my left, I saw nothing there. But I saw that the same ape (or some other ape) swing on the branches from the corner of my eye.

I tried to calm myself down and think it through. I got up and calmly started to crawl onto the branch towards the trunk of the tree so that I could slide down.

While crawling, I heard some moving of branches which I expected to be the ape.

I started to speed up. Just when I was about four or five feet away from the trunk of the tree, I heard a loud thud in front of me and I looked up.

As expected, I saw an ape in front of me. I started to back away slowly, trying not to seem to scared. I avoided eye contact with the ape.

But I couldn't resist the urge to look at him. When I looked at the ape, I realized that he was much smaller than the scarred ape. I assumed that this ape was not a very big one, and was very young.

The ape was some ten feet away from me, but I was still feeling scared.

The ape just took one gentle step towards me but I got scared and almost lost my balance.

I was just about to reach the end of the hammock when the ape said 'Relax, I won't kill you.'

Hearing this, I was awestruck to see an ape speaking to me. I just widened my eyes at the ape. I just stopped and took a deep breath and closed my eyes. I slapped myself a few times to make sure I was not sleeping.

'This is just a dream. You are not actually in front of a baby ape who just talked to you. You will just wake up some time and everything will be fine.'- I muttered to myself.

'Take a chill pill. First of all; I am not a baby ape, second; you are not dreaming and third; everything IS fine.'- said the ape and took another step closer to me.

'Hang on, don't come closer. I am already really scared of apes. I don't want any more injuries.'- I said.

'Okay, all right. I won't come closer. And an ape did that to you?'- asked the ape, staring at me up and down. 'I can't believe it. No one I know could be that dangerous.'- he said again. I was sure it was a 'he'.

'Anyways, get aside. I need to get out of here. I don't want to harm you.'- I said and started crawling towards the ape.

'You are safe here. You don't need to go anywhere. Plus, I need new friends. You look good enough, and also, I have some questions to ask you.'- said the ape.

I was listening to the ape but he pretended not hear anything what the ape said. I wanted a friend who would accompany and protect me. I wanted someone to talk to. I couldn't let go of this opportunity.

I was still crawling towards the ape with my hands and legs tightly wrapped around the branch.

Just then, a big splinter pierced right through the cloth which covered the wound on my right knee and into my skin, exactly on the place where the wound was the deepest.

A heartbeat later, I was hanging on the tree branch with my legs dangling some 600 feet above the ground.

The ape ran towards me and luckily caught me just before my hands slipped. The ape held me by the hand and put me on his back. I had the weird, tingly feeling of the day before when the scarred ape had me on his back.

'Hang on mate, and cover your head at all times.'- said the ape loudly before swinging a few branches to reach the ground.

I realized that the ape was trying to help me and befriend me. I had realized it a few minutes ago but chose to ignore it.

The ape gestured me to sit and I found myself obeying what the ape was saying.

The ape gently removed the cloth wrapped around my knee, where the splinter had been pierced through the skin.

'This will pain a bit.'- said the ape and pulled out the splinter from my leg.

I winced in pain but did not scream. 'Sorry.'- mouthed the ape.

'Why are you helping me?'- I asked and tried to stand up, but failed miserably. 'Because you are my friend.'- said the ape gently. I was still convincing my heart and mind to believe that apes could speak in this world.

I was surely touched by what the ape had said. *Because you are my friend*. Nobody had ever said that to me as I hardly had any friends at school and my nose was always buried in my books.

While the ape was still mending my wound by some plants and grass around me (whose names I didn't know), I looked at the Uganda Ironwood trees around me when I realized that they were almost the height of the redwood trees.

'Aren't these trees supposed to be a bit smaller in size.'- I asked quizzically, pointing to the Uganda Ironwoods.

'It's a long story.'- smiled the ape. 'Tell me, I have a lot of time.'- I said impatiently.

'Before starting with the long story, I would like to know your name.'- asked the ape excitedly. 'I'm Aiden, what's your name?'- I replied. 'Nice to meet you Aiden, I am Coco.'- said the ape, bringing his hand forward for a handshake.

I shook his hand. I had not realized how big Coco's hand was until I shook it. Coco's palm was around five or six times bigger than mine.

'Cute name.'- I said. 'Thanks.'- said Coco.

'So, Uhm... I have a question. I hope you won't feel bad.'- I said quietly. 'Yeah sure, you can ask me anything you want.'- said Coco politely. 'If you can ask me questions, even I will ask you questions.'- he said. 'Okay, but first I will ask.'- I said. 'That's fine with me. I am not in a hurry, unless you have anything else planned for the day.'- said Coco.

'No, I have nothing planned for the day except exploring this place.'- I said, brimming with excitement.

'Ok, are you ready for the Q&A?'- I asked.

'Yeah, and that was the first question.'- replied Coco playfully.

I chuckled slightly.

Coco helped me get up on my legs and they started strolling around, walking deeper and deeper into the forest, where no one would spot, interrupt or disturb us.

VIII

I ENTER THE DEVIL'S CAVE

Just strolling down the trees, dodging the sharp, pointy leaves; we were talking and laughing, and I must agree that Coco's sense of humor was pretty good for an ape.

'So, you mean that you learned to-', I said. 'That seems like a good place to sit and chat.'- said Coco interrupting me, and for the first time, I didn't feel offended when someone interrupted me. Usually, when Logan or handful of my nerd friends interrupt me; I feel like punching them in the face. I don't know why; I just feel like doing that. I hate when someone interrupts me.

But, in Coco's case, his voice was so calming and soothing that it was hard to imagine him getting angry or shouting at someone; for that matter to get annoyed at him.

Coco was pointing at a big rock. For a minute, I wondered how people (my bad, apes), could not spot us here. I thought how we could hide from the eyes of the apes.

After looking a bit more closely, I saw that he was not pointing at the massive rock; he was pointing at a cave right next to it.

I was not afraid of the dark, but I was surely claustrophobic.

But I couldn't object. After all, I couldn't see any other place where we could hide from the eyes of the gigantic apes. I followed Coco till we reached inside the cave.

I thought that the name 'Coco' was a funny but a cute name. Anyways, back to the story, the moment we sat inside the dark cave, the atmosphere changed. It turned cold and sunlight was totally blocked out. It was pitch dark.

I saw the figure of Coco, which looked creepy in the pitch darkness. Just then, Coco took out a lighter out of nowhere and lit a candle which was placed in the middle of us. That provided a bit warmth.

'Why,'- I started. 'Did I choose this place?'- Coco finished the sentence for me. I nodded my head.

'There is a story behind it. Only if you are ready to listen.'- said Coco calmly. I nodded impatiently.

'Only if you are so impatient.'- said Coco, understanding the impatience in my voice. 'If you have more questions, then feel free to-', he said.

'Ok, so my first question is: What is your age? Why did you choose this place?' He muttered something under his breath, which I was not able to hear as my voice was very loud for me to hear what he was saying. 'Why are you apes able to talk? Where am I?When am I going to go home? Is this just a dream or is this the reality? Buddy, no offence, but why is your name Coco and why the heck are you the size of King Kong?'- I said breathlessly, my eyes widened to its largest extent. Honestly, they were not the size of King Kong. I was just exaggerating it because they were huge. Okay, if King Kong is fifty feet, then these guys at least have to be forty or thirty-five.

Coco gave me time to catch my breath. I had no idea why my heart was pounding. I was helplessly panting, and I must appreciate the amount of patience he had.

Coco didn't seem to mind. 'None taken. Many apes make fun of my name; they always used to. I'm used to it.'- he said. I instantly regretted what I said and I understood that I had hit a nerve. 'Hey buddy, I'm really sorry, I didn't mean to hurt you. I am genuinely sorry.'- I said truthfully; my voice barely louder than a whisper.

'Anyways, do you have any more questions?'- asked Coco, changing the topic. Before I could answer, he said 'As you are only asking questions and not getting any answers.' And started to talk.

'First of all, why have I chosen this place? No ape dares to enter this cave.' Before I could ask 'Why', he said, 'This place is considered to bring misfortune to anyone who comes to this place. We believe that long ago; a merciless demon used to live here. His photos or assumption on how he would look are not present in our books as it is believed that his appearance is so scary that it would creep out the soul of anyone who looks at it. Anyways, our ancestors defeated the demon with all their force, millions were killed. We still believe that in some part of this cave, a part of his soul still exists in this cave and anyone who comes in here, that part of the soul attracts the ape by making it dream of all the happiness in the world becoming his, only if he frees the soul. As a result, the soul gets into the body of the ape. Once it has a host to live in, he gets more powerful every day, and once it gains power and rises out of the shadows, it will destroy anything that comes in its path and he will become unstoppable...'- ended Coco spookily.

His face was very close to mine. I was pretty sure that he could feel my warm and heavy breathing on his gigantic face.

'So, uhm... yeah, that's it. But don't worry Aiden, this is all fake. This story was told to us by our parents as children to keep us away from this cave as there are several bats and pointy rocks here. I guess there are scorpions and snakes as well. This was the main reason why we were told to stay away. The demon story was told to us so that we would not dare enter the cave.'- said the ape chilly.

'Don't other apes know this as well?'- I asked. 'If they know that this story of the demon is fake, why won't they come here? And won't they notice that you are missing?'- I continued to ask.

'Yes, the other apes do know that this story is fake, but they don't come here in fear of scorpions and snakes and bats and-' 'Yeah, I get it.'- I interrupted, wishing to hear no more. 'It's fine if you don't want to hear about what might be lurching right next to your leg, like:

snakes, lizards, cockroaches-' 'Ok! Ok! I get it. Just stop.'- I said a bit loudly.

I couldn't see his face clearly, but I could make out that he was teasing me. I sighed and chuckled.

Coco smiled and began again. 'This is gonna take a little longer than I thought.' I agreed and urged him to keep speaking.

'Sorry for this but I need some water, can I go and get some?'- asked Coco. 'Dude, you don't need permission from me to do anything, especially to drink water.'- I said, and honestly speaking; I never felt better talking to anyone.

In a few minutes' time, he was present in front of me and he had brought a glass of water for me as well. 'Thanks.'- I said and drank the water in one big gulp.

'Yeah, so I am fifteen.'- said Coco. 'And I'm fourteen.'- I said. Coco laughed and said 'That's cool.'

'Okay, so your next question was where are you. First of all, you are on earth.'- said Coco. Seeing my expression, he said 'Yeah, it's unbelievable. You are in the year 10972.'- he paused after as my jaw dropped open. I was lost for words.

'I've seen Dune 2 and that movie is set in 10191, and they are so advanced. Then how come you...', - I trailed off and didn't complete the sentence. 'Then how come we are not so advanced. For your information, Dune 2 is just a movie and it's in a whole different planet. This is Earth. We realized long ago that making development is not a bad thing but it's not a very good thing either. Pollution. Carbon dioxide. We apes are not greedy like humans. No offence.'- he said.

'None taken. But, buddy, Dubai already created flying cars.'- I said enthusiastically. 'I mean, yeah. That's old news for us.'- said Coco. I nodded.

Coco paused for a while and then continued. 'So, you might be wondering where all the humans are.'- he paused as I nodded my head and then continued. 'You see, so this happened a few centuries ago. As apes are the primitive relatives of humans, humans decided to do a little experiment on us. So, they implanted a chip in our brains which enhanced our intelligence and strength. The chip enabled us to speak and behave like humans. The chip had a side effect, which made us enormous in size. When our ancestors were completely developed with the chips, humans became afraid that we might grow stronger and more intelligent than them, and then overtake them. Hence, they started to make robots, and displayed them all over media saying that they will make our lives simpler and stuff like that. They never talked about us to the rest of the world. I think it might have already happened in your world that one of the robot's said that AI can run the world better than the humans. If you go back in 2024 and search up on google that will AI, take over the world. They would say yes but they will deny this fact. They would say that humans are very careful about their inventions. On media, they would display only one or two of their robots, but underground, they had an army of robots ready to attack whenever we got out of hand. But that never happened. As AI had predicted, they were going to take control of earth. The robots had been programmed to kill the apes. But one day, the scientist working on the robots messed something up which caused the robots to finish the apes as well as the humans. As you might have noticed that the robots were transformers. The robots finished all the humans and headed for the apes. The apes were losing miserably. But, one day, out of nowhere, some hundred more apes joined the fight and won against the robots. Which happened yesterday. Our scientists are still figuring out on how the apes joined the battle.'- ended Coco, lost in his own world.

'Typical human behavior.'- I muttered. 'Wait, you have scientists?'- I asked.

'Yeah, it's so cool right? No one knows where the lab is. We only know that there are scientists as they keep on giving reports to the king about some stuff. I may include discoveries about our pasts, or human's past, which they never discovered. We discovered civilizations before Mesopotamia. They were underwater, like the avatar. Can you believe that? We discovered plants which grew underground. Plants which do not require sunlight for photosynthesis. Even more astonishing, our scientists made a substance which can melt metal into a decomposable form.'- he said. 'Impossible dude. Just because I'm listening to you, that doesn't mean that you can tell me anything and I will believe that.'- I said, trying to provoke him. 'Listen Aiden, if you are trying to provoke me, or trigger my anger, you are failing miserably. You don't believe that these discoveries are true right?'- he said. 'Yes, I don't.'- I said.

I am not joking buddy, this is true. You don't believe it, go into the future and ask Coco yourself.

'Okay, what if I tell you that I know where the secret lab is?'- said Coco playfully. 'Impossible.'- I scoffed and crossed my arms. 'You don't believe me, then come get a look at it.'- said Coco. 'Before that, why is the lab a secret?'- I asked. 'Nobody knows but I do.'- said Coco. 'Now why is that so mister?'- I asked teasingly. 'I will not tell you until and unless you come with me.'- said Coco. 'Before that, you still need to answer the questions I asked you.'- I asked. 'Okay,'- said Coco impatiently for the first time. 'When are you going to go home, right.'- he said and paused for a while. 'Whenever you want to.'- he said. 'This is not a joke Coco. Anyways, have your scientists made a time machine?'- I asked. 'I don't know if they did or not.'- said Coco. 'Do you want to find out.'- I asked. I nodded my head. 'Then what are we waiting for?'- he asked.

With that, Coco was already at the cave's mouth. I ran towards Coco and said, 'Now it's your chance to ask questions to me.'- I said. 'Yeah fine, but first, I must show you the lab.'- he said restlessly.

IX

I LEARN SOMETHING ABOUT COCO

We exited the cave and started to walk towards the trees. 'Hey Coco,'- I said, breaking the silence between us. 'Yeah?'- he said. 'Where is this secret lab anyways?'- I asked. 'It's somewhere deep into the forest. Basically, we were never told about that part. No one ever had the curiosity to go beyond that point and explore except me.'- said Coco proudly. I put my hands in my pocket and started listening the sound of the chirping birds.

'Coco, are there any tailors or weavers here?' 'Yeah, there are a few. Why?'- he said. 'My clothes are very torn and not in a good condition. So, I need new ones.'- I said.

Coco nodded.

We were going deeper and deeper into the forest, away from ape civilization. Once again, I had the feeling of loneliness, except that Coco was there.

I had just met him, but it felt like I had known him for several years altogether. I felt as if I was walking all alone on Earth. Coco had never been so quiet before. He was always energetic and hyperactive. But right now, he was very focused. I felt that I was surrounded by land mines and one wrong step would risk our lives. I asked Coco, 'Hey, why are you so quiet?' 'Shh, this is one of the most protected areas of our kingdom. Coming here is banned. If the soldiers spot us, then we are in great trouble.'- he said, his voice barely louder than a whisper, as though scared that someone could be hearing us.

As though Coco read my mind, he said. 'Someone might be hearing us. It could be the soldiers or one of the civilians.'- he said quietly.

'The security here must be really tight.'- I said and Coco nodded. 'Then why did you come here, isn't there any other way which might lead to the lab?'- I asked.

'There is. There are two.'- he said in a whisper. 'Then why didn't we choose the other ones. The less the risk, more the better.'- I said quietly, following Coco.

'One goes through the palace. I know that one. There is another one, which goes underground and is not safe at all.'- he said.

'Are civilians allowed in the castle?'- I asked. Coco shook his head. 'Is there a one percent chance that you can sneak into the castle?'- I whispered. Coco shook his head once again. 'Not even at night?'- I asked. 'No.'- he gave a strained whisper, which clearly indicted me to shut up.

After a minute or two, I said 'Then how come you know the route which leads to the secret lab from inside the castle?'- I asked, struggling to keep my voice low.

Coco stopped abruptly and turned towards me. He said 'Because I'm the royal prince.'

Before I could process it. He said, 'Apes are coming, we need to hurry.' I knew that my hearing skills were really good but I couldn't hear anything.

Instead of running (or climbing), Coco grabbed my shirt and pulled me behind the dense bushes.

I opened my mouth to speak but he put a finger on his lips and moved some grass ahead of us, which was obstructing our view.

Coco made sure that we could see them but not them and to my surprise, I saw several apes in armors which I assumed to be the soldiers.

After a minute or two, the soldiers left and I was about to stand up when Coco pulled me down again. 'What now, they are gone!'- I said in a strained whisper.

Coco then pointed towards the left to see that the guards were hidden behind the trees, waiting for the victim to come out. I took a few deep breaths.

Then suddenly, I had the thought of me and Coco getting caught. I imagined Coco in the attire on a prince. I imagined him being excused as he was the prince and I being imprisoned. Or worst, as humans were already dead, they might drag me into the secret lab and do weird experiments on me. I imagined my legs and hands tied, weird-looking apes with crooked teeth staring at me. And then-

The thought of that made my skin tingle. I was safer with Coco. I still couldn't believe that a royal prince's name was 'Coco'. I mean, who in the world names a prince COCO?!

Anyways, back to the dark pathway, after two or three minutes, the guards left back to the palace and me and Coco continued on the same path. I wondered whether there were any CCTV's here, which were spying on us.

I shoved this thought away from my mind and started to follow Coco with all my concentration.

Just then, I thought about asking Coco if his real name was something else because Coco didn't seem like a prince name. Something like Charles III, or Naruhito, or- Okay, just leave it.

I noticed that this part had become quiet dark. I asked Coco why this was but he shushed me out. I thought that this was even more secured area.

I was adjusting my eyes to the darkness when I saw light in a distance. I became quite happy that we were now closer to our destination. Coco had also spotted the light and I could sense that he was starting to gather speed.

In a moment or so, we reached the light and Coco seemed to relax his shoulders.

We were just walking when I asked him 'So... wherever its dark, we need to keep our wits about and when its not dark, we don't need to stay alert, right?'

'I don't need to stay alert, but you need to at all costs as I can find some excuse to get away, but you...'- he paused and didn't finish the sentence, and I don't even want to know how it ended.

I was just about to ask something else when a foul smell blocked my nose and couldn't help from coughing.

'What is this?'- I asked and coughed once again. 'What is what?'- asked Coco, clearly not bothered by the foul smell.

'Buddy, this foul smell!'- I said, now breathing from my mouth to prevent the smell from reaching my insides. 'Oh this; we are near the dump yard. I'm used to this, just breathe from your mouth.'- he said. 'What do you think I am doing?'- I said.

I looked around and saw smoke coming from the dump yard.

'Hey, do you have any machines that work in the dump yard to recycle the waste?'- I asked Coco. 'No, all work is done by hand here.'- said Coco.

'Then what is that?'- I asked Coco, pointing towards the smoke. Coco looked towards the smoke and mouthed something.

'Dude, something might have burnt there. Come on, we are very close to the lab now.'- he said. 'But we need to check this out.'- I persuaded.

He opened his mouth to argue but the look on my face must have suggested that I was not going to listen to anything as he said 'Fine then. But not more than ten minutes. I don't want to stay there for long, makes me feel nauseous.'- he said. I a few moments, I was held by the collar of my shirt and I was being swinged towards the dump yard.

X
THERE'S SOMETHING MORE TO THE DUMP (beside the garbage and the foul smell)

'Why do we even need to go there?'- asked Coco, swinging both of us with only one hand (although the foul smell was getting to me after breathing from mouth, I was still persuading him to go further).

In two or three minutes, we were already inside the dump yard. Coco pointed towards the garbage while saying 'See, the garbage is burning. There's nothing to see here.' And then started walking out of the dump yard.

'Hang on Coco,'- I said. 'Now what Aiden, the smoke is clearly coming from the burning garbage.'- he said, a bit irritated.

I looked closely to see that there was something really wrong with the garbage, I just couldn't figure it out. I stepped closer and tried to take a banana peel from the pile, but my hand went right through it.

I called Coco and asked him to take a look at it and said 'This is an illusion. I told you that the smoke was not coming from the garbage.'

'You never said that to me.'

'I just did. Now, are you willing to delve deeper into this mystery?'

'No.'

With that, we walked right through the burning garbage.

The scene there was shocking, and you won't believe me if I told you. But you have no other option than to believe me, do you?

So, I was seeing robots (I don't want to make it dramatic, like- I was seeing twenty feet long creatures who were prepared to finish this war for once and for all and blah, blah, blah).

'Robots?!'- exclaimed Coco. 'How are they alive?'- I muttered. 'God knows.'- he said. 'We need to figure this out.'- I said. 'WE!? I am so out of this. It's only you. I need to tell this to father.'- said Coco, terrified. 'Coco, do you think anyone will believe us if we say that the robots are still alive and they are building a whole army in the dump yard! Everybody is still recovering from the war and no one wants to fight just after a day of rest.'- I said.

Coco folded his hands and nodded. 'But how did they manage to build such a big army in a day?'- he asked me. 'That's what we need to figure out.

I looked around, me eyes searching for a clue that could help me understand this.

Just then, my eyes fell on three robots, who seemed to be fighting about something. I don't know why but I had a feeling that I could find something there. As I watched, one of them took out a knife-like-thing and stabbed one of the others and that guy turned into ashes right in front of me, but one shiny thing remained. As I focused my eyes a bit more, I saw that only a shiny thing remained.

When I squinted my eyes a bit mzore, I saw that the shiny object was none other than a chip, the chip which I saw when I first came into the future.

After two or three minutes, a layer started to form on the chip, slowly, it turned back into a robot, and the robot walked away casually as if nothing happened.

A re-generating chip. I must say that the robots were very smart. After all, we were the ones who built it, and we were the people who were responsible for the end of humankind.

I told Coco about it. Without wasting time, me and Coco left the dump yard as soon as we could.

'We need to tell this to father as soon as we can.'- Coco said. 'Do you think that he will believe us?'- I asked. 'No, but we can try.'- said Coco, clearly giving no false hopes.

***

The palace was magnificent. Although it was made up bricks, it was stunning. The architecture was magnificent. A red flag on the top of the tower, indicating victory. The walls of the palace looked unbreakable. The walls of the palace were painted with shades of brown. Carvings of mythical creatures was delicately etched into the walls. Creatures like chimeras, dragons, griffins, sirens, mermaids, basiliks, minotaur, bigfoots and chupacabras. They almost looked alive. The whole palace looked very welcoming. They were all surrounded by precious stones like, diamonds, rubies, yellow and blue sapphires, obsidian and several more. The windows were enormous. They were dome shaped glass windows which were stained. The light of the sun reflected beautifully off the windows and the stones. The whole palace glowed a golden-yellow colour.

Okay, so we entered the palace only because Coco was there.

Soldiers were staring at us. Most probably because Coco was there with a human (almost a hundred times smaller than them), who were gone extinct decades ago.

In a few moments, we were waiting behind massive doors made up of woods. We were standing there, waiting to be called in by the king.

I was getting anxious; I was wondering several things at once. Just then, I felt the doors moving; they were opening. I could not waste a second, I needed to warn these giants about the robots. They could attack anytime now.

But even Coco could do that. I was just a witness of the accident. First of all, I didn't even know the way I was supposed to talk to a king. What if I said something and they misinterpreted my words? What if I become their prisoner? What is their king were mean and strict?

I was calming myself down. You know how bad I am at that. I was just overthinking. I was just nervous, that's all.

Just then, the gates opened and Coco started to walk inside. I don't know what happened tome but his way of walking completely changed. His left hand was behind his back and right was by his side. Coco's body language was no longer like a normal teenager, he started behaving like a prince. His back was as straight as a line.

I decided to follow him. I put my left hand behind my back and right hand was placed by my side.

I was aware of the eyes following me. I couldn't help looking around hall, or whatever that is called. Maybe a meeting area? I was humongous. Twelve ministers were seated on my right and twelve on my left. I wondered why the king needed so many ministers.

Just then, Coco stopped abruptly, causing me to bump into him. I hurried to his left. Coco bowed deeply, and so did I. He said, 'Greetings father.' 'Not father. It's *Your majesty*.'- said the king.

'Forgive me your majesty.'- said Coco. 'Say it again.'- said Coco's father in a deep and stern voice.

Coco hesitated for a while and said 'Greeting your majesty.' I could sense that he was kind of scared from his father.

Without wasting a moment, I bowed deeply and said 'Greetings your majesty.' As loudly as I could. 'There's no need to shout, I am not deaf.'- said the king loudly.

Coco looked at me as if telling me to ignore his father and not take his words seriously. It forced me to wonder how a son and a father could be so different.

Coco looked up and so did I. 'What happened Coco, why have you come here? What is so important that you needed to spoil our celebration of victory over the robots.'- he said bitterly, trying to control his urge to kick Coco and me out of this hall immediately.

'I am sorry to disturb your celebration; but this is important.'-said Coco.

XI

I MAKE THE KING ANGRY

The king sighed and rested his back on his throne, as if giving less importance to whatever Coco was going to say. 'Me—', began Coco, but was interrupted by the king, 'Why do you have a human with you? They were gone extinct years ago, then how- Wait, did you by chance get your hands on the time machine and teleported him to the future, Coco!?'- he said and pointed towards me with a disgusted face.

'No, he came here all by himself. I don't know how he came here; I didn't ask him.'- said Coco, staring right into the eyes of his father.

The king then looked at me, his eyes searching me for an answer. There was a weird silence that made me feel awkward. I felt as if eyes were piercing right through me.

Just then, Coco broke the silence, catching everyone's attention, and the eyes were now on him; I was thankful to him for that.

'I am present here to tell you that the robots are still alive, and are building an army in the dump yard. We need to act soon or else we can die. This time, the forces need to be stronger; as the opponent's army is much bigger.'- said Coco confidently.

There was a moment of silence before everyone burst into laughter; including the king. They treated this as a joke. They kept laughing for a few minutes; until, I stepped front and said with all the courage I had, 'Coco is not lying, I have seen it myself. If you don't believe us, come see yourself; but if you don't come, I will assume that you are too lazy to come. If you don't want to come, you have no option but to believe us. I am a witness.' And looked at Coco, who had a sparkle in his eye. I came back and stood by his side. I patted him on the back gently.

I looked up at the king, and I got the answer almost immediately. 'Extinct creature, you are not a witness; you merely are a friend of Coco and are just fooling around. You are a kid.' He said and laughed at me.

I clenched my fists so hard that when I looked at my hand, there was a thin line of blood. I looked up, my eyes full of hatred and frustration. I was angry at the humiliation Coco and I faced. I was so angry that I couldn't keep it in. I hardly knew what I was saying, 'You idiot! Why don't you understand that this is important? You think that we are just fooling aaround? I'm sorry, but we aren't stupid to come all the way from the dump yard to the court to lieand fool around. I don't care if you believe it or not, that's up to you. Its your choice whether you want to listen to us or not. I'm telling you for the last time, listen to us and stop wasting time, or fall to your face in front of the robots.'- I said shouted angrily and eyed every minister present in the court angrily. To my surprise, I saw the scarred ape present in the court. I realized that he was the king's minister.

I stared at the king angrily. Everyone was left speechless, including the king. I was panting heavily.

I looked at the king one last time, my eyes gleaming with hatred. I looked at Coco and pulled him by his hand; and started to stomp towards the doors.

I was feeling angry, frustrated, annoyed and irritated all at once. I had a lot of patience but I don't know why when the king laughed at Coco, I felt angry and couldn't hold back. Coco looked like he was hit by lightning. 'Aiden, I don't think that this is a good idea.'- he said. 'What is not a good idea?'- I asked. 'Just storming out of the courtroom like this.' he said. 'Why? What's wrong with it? They insulted you, Coco. How do you not feel bad about it?' -I asked. 'You don't need to worry about me. I'm used to this now.' He said.

We were just about to exit when two soldiers came and blocked our path. 'Aiden,' Coco began. 'I think we should turn back.'- he said. He turned back and looked front again. 'There are more behind.'- he said. I looked behind to find some fifteen soldiers with spears pointing right at us. I took a deep breath and gulped the lump that had formed in my throat.

'I should not have said whatever I said.' I spoke, regretfully.

Coco nodded. 'On the count of three, we run forward as fast as we can and try to dodge the soldiers in front of us.'- I whispered. 'That's a very bad plan.'- said Coco nervously. 'Do you have any better ideas?'- I asked. He did not say anything; so, I took the answer as 'no'.

'One... two...', my voice got stuck in my throat when I found out that Coco was not beside me. My courage and anger faded away as I saw Coco being forcefully taken away from me. The soldiers held him tightly in a corner.

As my attention got diverted to Coco, two soldiers grabbed me and dragged me and threw me right in the center of the court.

As I tried to stand up and fight back, the soldiers held me down. I had absolutely no power to fight back giants. I looked like a small toy in their hands.

I looked up and saw the king coming down the steps with his cape lightly brushing the ground. Up closer, he looked even more majestic. He was wearing a golden armor which had a roaring tiger etched in black to the center and was facing sideways. He was wearing long golden boots which had several detailed designs. His cape looked like a sky full of stars. It was pitch black with sparkly white stars. He wore a golden locket which made a weird and complicated symbol and it was fitted inside a circular boundary. A golden chain hanged around his neck which held the locket.

He came near me and looked down at me with a disapproving; disappointed look. He bent down to whisper in my ear, 'Kid, you did a *very, very* big mistake. You picked the wrong person to mess with.'

The last line sent a cold shiver up my spine. He stood up straight with his hands behind his back and looked at the soldiers who were holding me. 'Finish him.'- he said and gave a cold chuckle at me. With that, he turned and climbed the steps to comfortably sit on his throne.

XII

I BECOME A MESSIAH OUT OF NOWHERE

I heard Coco struggling to escape the tight grip of the soldiers. Two more soldiers came in front of me with their spears pointing right at my heart. I closed my eyes and got ready to face death anytime now.

'You still didn't answer my question.'- said the king in a loud voice. I must have looked very confused, he said 'How did you come here?'- he said through gritted teeth.

'Oh,'- I said, 'through this.' And raised my left hand to reveal the golden watch.

I looked at the king and he looked like he was struck by lightning. I looked around the court to see that the scarred ape's eyes had widened and jaw was dropped open.

For a moment, I was shocked myself when I saw the scarred ape going on his knees and bending down to me. I looked around to see that the ministers got up from their seats and bowed down to me. The soldiers who were holding me now took a step back and bowed down to me. I looked at the corner where Coco was there to ask him what all this was about. To my surprise, the guards had left Coco and all three of them were bowing down to me. I looked at the king who was also bowing down to me.

The next moment, I had several questions in my mind which needed to be answered immediately. Like- Why was everyone bowing down to me? Why did everyone seem so thunderstruck when I showed them the watch? Was this watch of great importance to them? And stuff like that.

I guess we're both wondering what this drama is about. Well, I know what this drama is about; so, let me tell you.

'Why are you all bowing down to me? Just a minute ago, you were trying to kill me, now you are bowing down to me. What's the matter?'- I asked.

'Are you telling me that you have absolutely no idea about the significance of this watch?'- asked the king and gave a weird hand gesture to one of the soldiers behind me. 'No.'- I said.

The soldier whom the king had given the gesture to came towards me and for a heartbeat, I thought that they were going to make me a prisoner and torture me to death. Fortunately, that didn't happen.

The soldier held my hand and tried to take out the watch from my hand. But the watch didn't come out of my hand (as expected). The soldier shook his head and looked down. He stepped back to align himself with the other soldier. I looked at the king and his expression said 'This is impossible. It's a miracle.'

'What is the significance of this watch?'- I asked. Before anyone could answer that. The king was about to answer but I don't know why; I couldn't contain myself and my feelings got blurted out of my mouth even before I could stop them. 'Listen, if this watch is important for you, then take it. I don't want it. Just fix this thing and let me go back. I want to meet my mother. Please, just take this thing off me. I was just a normal teenager who was playing video games and reading books. But from the time this thing has come into my life, it has turned my life upside down. Yesterday, I almost go killed by that guy. It was a miracle that I am somehow still alive. See, this thing is not coming off.'- I said.

'Listen, you can't go back. You got that watch because of a reason. You are here among us because of a reason. You are our messiah for a reason.'- said the king. 'WHAT?!'- I exclaimed almost immediately. 'Me; a messiah. Enough of this drama. If you are kidding, this is a really bad joke. Even if you are telling the truth, give me one reason you are not trying to kill me. Give me one reason why I should believe you. Give me one reason and I will agree that I am your messiah. I mean, messiahs are supposed to be strong and confident and look at me. I hate to agree but I am neither very strong nor confident. You guys are hundred times my size. I should ask you guys to protect me, and you are asking me to protect you? You can trample me or break all my bones with just a flick of your hand.'- I said.

At this point, I actually wanted to go home. I wanted to go home so bad.

'I know this is hard, kid.'- said the king, a sudden change in his voice.

'I know that there are a lot of questions in your mind, and I can understand. Even I had.'- said the king. 'Wait a second, you were a messiah too?!'- I asked, puzzled. 'Yes child, even I was a messiah. I just didn't have the watch at that time. Only my great-great grandfather had it. Everyone in our family has an advantage above all to become a messiah. To become one, you must pass a test. Which only five percent of the apes can pass.' he said

Before he could continue, I asked 'Then how come you—', I began,

'I get it. How come I became the king if I was the messiah? There is a believe that after the messiah does something to protect us, he or she has to battle the king. Willingly, or unwillingly. If the messiah successfully beats the king, then he becomes the king.'- said the king, staring right into my eyes.

The thought of battling the king made me shiver. As though the king read my mind, he said 'Don't worry kid, you don't need to battle me as you are not an ape. We could never imagine a human becoming a messiah.'- said the king gloomily.

'Neither could I.'- I muttered.

'Anyways,' began the king. 'The watch was lost after my great-great grandfather died and it was never found... until now. Soon, it became a tale among the people. It was then when the test for the messiah began. It is believed that whoever has the watch; is the messiah and needs no test to be passed. Furthermore, there are chances that some apes want to take wrong advantage of the watch. Uhm... you see, if you have the watch, you don't need to do the test, and a messiah is considered superior to everyone, including the king. So, everyone has to obey and follow the orders of the messiah.'- said the king. 'So—', I began. 'Let me continue, questions later, messiah.'- he said.

Messiah, the word had so much respect given to it by the king. I felt as though the weight of the world had been put on my shoulders. They were expecting me to guide them to victory. But, how could I. I mean, I was just a teenager who liked playing video games and got bullied in school. How could I? What if I failed them? What if I wasn't able to-

Okay, let's just get to the main point, shall we?

'So,'- began the king, 'Now how do we understand whether the messiah has evil intentions or good? The—',

'I hope there isn't any other tests.'- I interrupted.

The king sighed. 'No, there aren't any tests. Anyways, if the watch comes out of the messiah's hand, then the he has evil intentions. But if not, the messiah has a golden heart and has been born to guide us.'- said the king.

Before I could say anything, the king said 'What is your name?' and shifted on his throne. 'My name's Aiden, your majesty.'- I said. 'Not your majesty, only Richard.'- said the king.

There were several gasping and surprised expressions on the word 'Richard'.

'Aiden, come up here for a minute.'- he said; and for a moment my stomach did a backflip, then a front flip, and then a somersault.

I slowly walked up the steps and stood right in front of the king. He leaned a bit closer and whispered in my ear 'Messiah, this is a very big responsibility, so take seriously. We rely on you. We give our lives in your hand. Listen, many apes will talk behind your backs. Just ignore them. Listen to me. I know you don't know how to organize an army and their positions. I know you don't know any war strategies; I will guide you Sire.'- he said and leaned back on his throne.

'Um... please don't call me sir, sire, or messiah. It feels weird, and I feel like I have a responsibility on my shoulders. Allow me to call you "your majesty". I don't want to call you by your name.'- I said. 'Whatever you feel is comfortable messi- Aiden.'- he said and smiled.

I hurried down a few steps but came up again. 'Your majesty, no offence; but is Coco's real name so or is it something else?'- I asked and the king chuckled at this.

'No, no. His real name is not Coco. It's just a pet name. He doesn't like his real name and feels like it is very, very royal. His real name is Colson.'- he said. 'Colson told me not to tell it to anyone and keep it a secret. But as you are our mess— '

'No. You will not treat me special just because I am your messiah. Treat me like any other ape.'- I said and ran down the steps.

I was just going to exit when I turned and asked the king, 'Can Coco come with me?'

The king made another weird; complicated gesture and the soldiers freed Coco. He came running towards me and we both left the courtroom together.

XIII

I GET SOME NEW CLOTHES

'Hey,'- I said. 'Your father isn't that bad after all.'

'Oh, look who's saying it. You called him a fool and a king not worthy of a throne.'- said Coco and laughed. 'Dear Colson, let— '.

'Dad told you, my name.'- he said. 'I told him not to tell it to anyone. Now you can tease me.'

'Right. So, Colson…', - I began teasingly, 'let the past remain in the past. Live your present and plan your future.'- I said. Coco did a fake yawn and we both laughed.

'Hey, after you became the messiah, you will mostly be busy planning war strategies and attack formations and blah, blah, blah. We won't be able to spend time together; especially when the robots are about to attack God knows when.'- said Coco gloomily.

'Hey, I will spend time with you, like I'm doing now. Look, we've just left the palace. It's hardly been five minutes since we left the palace. We will at least have half an hour or one hour before they call me to do "blah, blah, blah".'- I said.

Like always, I had spoken too soon.

Just then we heard a voice. We turned to see a soldier hurrying towards us. 'Like I said. Now off you go, messiah.'- sad Coco sadly.

'It's okay. We'll take a whole day to chat and do some fun when the battle is over.'- I said and ran towards the soldier.

'Messiah, the king is calling you.'- he said loudly. I could sense that he was a bit nervous. 'Hey, no need to call me *messiah*. Just call me Aiden; and loosen up a bit, will you?'- I said and walked ahead of him.

I heard some sighing noises and then rushing footsteps. The soldier caught up with me and said, 'His majesty wants you to wear new clothes. An attire for messiah.'

'An *attire*?! I mean, is that necessary?'- I asked. 'I can't do anything, it's a ritual.'- he said. 'Uhm... I have a question. How did they make clothes for me so fast? I mean, if it were an ape who became a messiah; it was still understandable. You know like, there are some clothes for a messiah, but me?'- I asked.

'Yeah buddy, I know you didn't understand what I said. Don't worry, even I don't know what I just said.'- I paused. I knew I made the situation a bit awkward. 'I mean, there must be some spare clothes kept in a locker for the messiah. See, I'm so tiny. How did they end up making clothes my size so quickly?' I asked

'Oh, uhm... yeah. There are spare clothes for a messiah; always available for them. But I'm not quite sure how they prepared clothes your size so quickly.'- he said.

We had now reached the gates of the palace.

The soldier did a series of knocks on the gate and backed away. After a few seconds, the door opened and we entered the palace.

I wondered why this "series of door knocks" didn't take place during the time me and Coco entered the palace. I guessed that there were some CCTV cameras which allowed the door to open only for Royal blood.

Anyways, when we entered the 'Great' court of the apes, two soldiers were holding a plate-kind-of-thing in their hands (Most probably a big tray).

I saw the king smiling down at me.

I wondered what kind of clothes I had to wear. I seriously was in no mood to wear some linen clothes with shorts or some big necklaces. I wondered if they expected me to wear some earring, because I didn't have an ear piercing and I was in no mood to do one.

So, there's this incident after which I never want to do an ear piercing or any piercing of any kind because of my brother. Okay, so what happened was that my brother left his headphones in my room. You see, he came to my room to *borrow* a book of mine, who he hasn't returned to me till now. A novel, one of my favorites. I went to his room to return his headphones and I found him doing a nose piercing on his own without telling mum. I honestly don't want to describe that scene to you.

Just so that you know, this happened some three years ago and just after some three days of the incident, I slipped on a paper (because I was running) and when I took that paper to throw it into the dustbin, I found out that it was page 47 from the novel Logan 'borrowed' from me.

Sorry, I got diverted from the topic. My bad.

The king came towards me and whispered in my ear, 'Don't worry kid; this is not some very lengthy robes, nor these clothes will make you feel cold.'

'Cold?'- I asked. 'It's not that cold.'- I said and sneezed loudly. 'Sorry.'- I said, and sneezed again. 'Dust—', one more sneeze, 'Allergy.'- another sneeze.

The king chuckled. Sneeze. 'You don't have dust allergy kid. It *is* cold out there. It's twelve degrees out there at three in the afternoon. Weather forecast say that it is most probably to start snowing from tomorrow night, and will continue to snow heavily until next week. They say snow will pile up to seven feet.'- he said.

'Seven feet?!'- I exclaimed and the king nodded.

The king's outfit had changed from what he was wearing some five minutes ago.

I noticed that the king was wearing a woolen jacket which seemed quite warm. He didn't wear his gold armor but he was still wearing his golden locket. He was no longer wearing his cape as the woolen coat was as big as the cape. He wore long black boots which came a bit below the knees.

Suddenly, I shivered and I didn't even realize when I folded my arms and gritted my teeth.

The king's expression said 'just agree that you are feeling cold.'

So, without wasting any more time, I accepted the clothes and bowed to the king.

I was just about leave when the king stopped me and said, 'Follow the soldiers. They will guide you to the dressing room.'- he said.

'There's a dressing room?!'- I asked, surprised.

I thought that royal people were supposed to change in their own rooms. I mean, I could never even think that

As though the king read my mind, he said, 'We have dressing rooms for guests.'

I was just about to leave when the king stopped me again, 'Listen Aiden, they will guide you to dressing room sixteen. Once they are gone, move on to room 20, you'll find it easily. Go to room 20, I have a little surprise for you. Now go on, the soldiers are waiting. One more thing, don't open the clothes until you reach room 20.'- he said and smiled at me.

'I have this question, uhm... why do you always wear this locket? I mean you changed your whole outfit except the locket. You didn't take out the locket.'- I said.

'This. The chain was given to me by Coco on his fourteenth birthday. He made it by himself, and the locket; every king has to wear it during court meetings. I never usually never take out the locket as it is very hard to put it back, do I don't do it. Rarely. But the chain, I never take it out. If an enemy asks for the chain, I will give my life instead. I am always scared that it will get lost. I will never, never until I die; take this chain out.'- he said.

He looked at me and his eyes gestured me to go with the soldiers.

Without waiting for another minute, I hurried after the soldiers with the clothes in my hand.

While walking, I took a look at my clothes to find linen clothes.

I gave a disappointed sigh and followed the soldiers till the door of room 16.

Even the door was worth appreciating. It had room 16 labelled on the top, in small font. But what captured my attention was the thing written in the middle.

There was 'Aiden' written in the middle in big, designer gold letters. Below 'Aiden' was written 'The Messiah' in a smaller font, which was bigger than 'room 16'.

As told by the king, I waited till the soldiers were gone, pretending to tie my laces.

I made sure that the soldiers were far away before I made my way to Room 20.

I reached the door and I opened it easily. When I went inside, the view was indescribable.

My first task was to search for the surprise. I love surprises. So, I love them because once my- sorry.

I looked around and saw a box placed on the floor which was wrapped very neatly. It was placed on the doorstep. I picked up the box with one hand and read the note on it. 'For Aiden'. There was one more note on the clothes which he had not seen before; it read 'open when after you find the surprise.

I didn't understand it at first, the clothes were not packed for me to open them.

Then, when I looked closely, I saw that the linen was just a wrapping, there was something more inside.

But before opening the clothes, I saw another note on the same place where the previous note had been, on the box.

It said, 'Open me and the surprise when you go back to room 16.

I lazily opened the door and

I couldn't believe my eyes. The room was amazing. The tiles were made up of crystal-clear white marble. There was a humongous glass chandelier hanging right above the center of the room. It had several scented candles in it which smelled amazing. There was a comfortable-looking rocking-wooden chair placed right next to the warm fireplace beside the mirror. The window wall which showed the beautiful environment of the kingdom was on the right side of the room. The view was beautiful. There was a mirror which was decorated with gems like ruby and sapphire.

There was a cozy-looking and warm bed ready for me. The bed was located right adjacent to the window wall. There was a small table next to the bed, where I would keep my novels at home before sleeping. There was also a heater in the room and the warmth of the room was giving me a very comfortable and at-home feeling.

I took out my combat boots and closed the door. It was then when I realized how bad was the condition of my boots. My right boot was all worn off and the sole was separated from the rest of the shoe. My left boot was torn at several places and the lace had vanished from the boot.

It looked withered, torn and old although it had only been five months since I brought them.

I put them aside and advanced towards the bed with my clothes and the surprise.

I opened the linen clothing to find new and fresh clothes. I gathered them in my hands and quickly changed.

***

I was astonished at how perfectly the clothes had fit me. I looked absolutely flawless in it.

I was wearing a dark-wash jeans with a black denim jacket and a white cotton t-shirt under it. I wondered how this would keep me warm. I couldn't understand how jeans, a white cotton shirt and and denim jacket could keep me warm. I mean, I looked amazing and it perfectly matched my curly light brown hair. I mean how could one look so good-

Sorry for getting diverted from the topic again. So, I could always figure it out later. Anyways, it was time to open the surprise.

I put the surprise on my bed and started to unbox it. Inside, there was a shoe box; whose name I couldn't read as it was written in some alien language, which I assumed to be the language used by the apes.

Excitedly, I opened the box to reveal black combat boots. It was the new and upgraded version of mine. It had an army look to it. It was beautiful. To my surprise, it had a pair of new and warm socks in it.

Without waiting for another moment, I put on the socks and then the boots. The overall look was amazing. I never wore such fancy and branded cloths, neither I had any interest in it.

Honestly, if I wore this to school or in any other place such as malls. I was sure that people would call me a self-obsessed teenager.

I was just admiring myself in the mirror when I heard a knock on the door.

I hurried towards the door and peeped it open to find the king at my door.

I made myself look as confident and majestic as I could. Although the king was doing nothing to look like one, he still looked majestic and very king-like with his hands behind his back.

He entered the room and sat on the bed. I closed the door in a hurry and sprinted to stand in front of the king.

'Sit down.'- he said. His voice harsh and stern like before. He never talked to me like that after the incident in the court. A few minutes ago, he had kindness and sweetness in his voice. I wondered how people's behavior changes so quickly.

I sat down and noticed that the king was not wearing his locket, which I found odd. He wasn't even wearing his chain, which made me a bit suspicious.

'I see you have changed into new clothes.'- he said in a king-like manner. He was sitting with his back straight and his hands clasped together.

I nodded lightly as I couldn't find any other appropriate reply that didn't feel awkward.

'Very well then Aiden. I want you in my room after fifteen minutes. Exactly after fifteen minutes. Not fifteen minutes one second, or fourteen minutes fifty-nine seconds. I hope that it's clear.'- he said and I nodded like an obedient dog.

He stood up, even I stood up; and opened the door. Just when he was about to leave, I opened my mouth to ask what was wrong and what is the problem and if there was anything I could do to solve it. I also wanted to add, why are you so grumpy? Judging by his expression and mood, I decided not to say it. Then I decided not to say anything.

I knew that there was something wrong with the king. I assumed that he got some news about the war. That must have upset him.

I closed the door once he left and sighed heavily. I went and sat down on my bed, took out my combat boots and put my legs inside the warm blanket. I looked outside the window, admiring the beauty of nature. It was raining heavily and the smell of the rain on the mud was reaching me, urging me to fall asleep.

I was quite sure that I couldn't stay up for more time. I couldn't believe that it was only yesterday that I came in here and almost died, and today, I was a messiah.

I smiled to myself and my eyes drifted away from the window and onto my pillow. My head touched the pillow without my will and I continued to see the scenery with my eyes which were already half-shut. Lying down on my bed made me realize how much sleep my body had needed. But I knew I couldn't fall asleep yet. I had to go meet the king.

I turned my back towards the window and I saw that a mug of hot chocolate was kept on the table beside my bed; which I knew was not there before.

XIV
I DRINK A CUP OF HOT CHOCOLATE WHICH I SHOULDN'T HAVE DRANK

As I didn't want to sleep, I drank the whole thing... in one single gulp.

My fourth mistake.

After drinking the hot chocolate, I suddenly felt sleepier. I scratched the back of my head and went to the washroom to wash my face.

I checked the watch for the time; but the watch was stuck.

There was a watch on the wall that showed the time as 3:31, and I remembered that the king came at around 3:25.

I wore my new combat boots and opened the door to leave my room. That's when a thought struck me. I didn't know where the king's room was.

Amazing. I thought.

I decided that I would ask someone where his room was. With that thought, I closed the door of my dressing room and fortunately, I saw a soldier only a few meters away.

I ran up to him and asked, 'Hi, do you know where the king's room is?'

'Yes. Do you want me to guide you there?'- he asked. 'Sure. Thank you.'- I said and he guided me to the king's room.

After a minute or two of walking, he said, 'There. That one.' And pointed towards a room whose door was decorated with several gems; like ruby, diamond, sapphire and several more whose name I can't recall.

I knocked on the door, not knowing if I came before time or after time.

After a moment, the door opened to reveal the king; standing majestically in front of me.

I entered through the door and the king locked it in a hurry just after I'd entered.

I thought that this was weird but I put that thought aside and sat down a chair.

The room was the same as mine but a bit bigger.

After a few heartbeats, the king sat down on the chair next to me and stared at me, staring me up and down.

I found this really weird. I didn't give importance to this, which was my mistake as I still had time.

I was waiting for the king to start a conversation as I grow really impatient during these awkward silences. The silence was only awkward for me, not for him; which I could sense from his body language.

He stared at me as though he expected me to tell him that I had some superpowers like I could read minds or anything.

I expected him to say something and he expected me to say something. I thought.

So, I decided to start a conversation. But I was still thinking what I could say to start a conversation between us. I thought about saying something about planning war strategies. I was almost expecting him to say that the robots are going to attack and I needed to lead them.

Well, I already knew that.

I started a conversation by saying something like this, 'Uhm... I liked your surprise. I love these combat boots. I wanted them badly as my old ones had torn apart. Actually, I needed them.'- I said awkwardly.

I expected him to say *I'm glad you liked it.*

But what he said was, 'Did you drink the hot chocolate placed on the table?'

'Yes.'- I replied.

By then, the king was staring into my sky-blue eyes with his dark, intense, stern and majestic brown eyes. I don't know how; but I somehow found the courage to stare back into those.

He stood up, leaned closer to me and squinted his eyes to stare deeper into mine.

Then, he sat down again and asked, 'Very well then. Then that should be some five more minutes.'- he said, checking his watch.

I knew that the king was not like this. I knew that that was not the king's voice. Wait a minute, was he the *real* king; or just a *doppelgänger*?

I knew that this was not the real king. I could make it out.

The doubt I had in my mind which said that something about the king was wrong; now was no longer a doubt.

I looked at the door to see that it was locked. Making a run for it would be completely stupid as he was faster, stronger and bigger than me.

I think he saw me looking towards the door because he said, 'Don't even think about it. I'll just reach out to you with my hand and pull you back here. It's not worth trying.'

For a moment, I thought that he could read minds but the next moment, that thought seemed foolish.

'What do you want from me?'- I asked, coming straight to the point.

'Finally, you asked it.'- he said 'It took you a long time to realize that you are not *worthy* of being a messiah.'

I remembered that I had said to him that he was not worthy of the throne. I think he was taking revenge for that.

The thought that he was not the real king came back to me.

Then, all of a sudden, I had another thought.

What if it was the real king and all along, he was pretending to be nice? What if he wanted to kill me? What if he had already realized that I was not worthy of being the messiah? What if-

My thought process was broken by the king, 'Everybody believes in you. Everybody thinks that *you* will guide them to victory. What a pity.'- he said, mocking pity. 'But,'- he said, a sudden change in his voice; a voice filled with hatred and annoyance. 'Who will guide them if the messiah is gone? Dead?'- he said in a robotic tone and put his hand on my shoulder; except that it wasn't a hand.

And then, what happened next scared the hell out of me.

The king put his hand on his forehead, grabbed the skin and pulled it out. Inside, it was a robot.

I wanted to shout and call for help. I didn't even know if anyone was around to hear me. I didn't even know whether the real king knew that he had a clone in the palace.

What if the king had already known this and the robot finished him?

No, that could not have been possible. No, no, no...

I had to kill him. But how?

Suddenly, I felt a throbbing pain in my forehead. That pain was so immense that it made me wince.

Imagine a metal bottle came and hit you at a speed of sixty kilometers per minute. Now triple the pain.

The robot had seen my pain. He- my bad, it said, 'Amazing, two minutes are left.'- he- it said.

'What did you put in that hot chocolate?'- I asked through gritted teeth as I doubled over in pain as I fell on the ground. My whole body ached.

'Zeprelataine Dieropaloli venom X.'- it said and for a heartbeat; I forgot all about my pain and gave a confused look at the robot.

'What?'- I asked.

It was hard to read his expression. Sorry, it was a robot. It had *no expression.*

'Zeprelataine Dieropaloli venom X.'- it said again, annoyed.

'Uh huh, but I'm still confused. Is it zepralaten or zipritalaine or...', I said.

'Shut up kid or else I'm going to kill you right here!'- it shouted.

'Anyways I'm going to die because of this zepre thing. It doesn't make a difference.'- I muttered.

'One minute left.'- it said.

'Wait a minute, what—'

'You have only a minute left.'

'What is this Zepre thing anyways?'

'It's a venom. A venom developed by us; which can kill any ape, and human's DNA is very similar to that of apes. Thus, you're dead. So, any last words?'

'My last wish, tell me how you guys die.'

'Uhm... just because you are dying. Otherwise, I wouldn't have told you this. There are two ways in which we can die. First: you have to hit right in the middle of the chest to destroy the chip. Second: There's a kill code. If you install that on the master computer, all the robots will die immediately and there's no coming back and the kill code is-'

Perfect timing, I close my eyes and I don't hear what the kill code is.

XV

I OWN A MAGICAL WEAPON

The next thing I know is that I'm still alive and I'm closed in a very small room. Actually, it looked as though it was a closet. I didn't have space to breathe or even move.

On that happy note, my eyes; mouth; legs, and hands were tied.

As I've mentioned before; I'm claustrophobic. Just amazing, right? Best day of my life.

I tried to open the knot of my hands, but no luck. The knots on my legs and hands were so tight that they blocked the flowing blood. I wouldn't have survived if one of these knots were on my neck.

I was lying there; helpless.

While trying to open the knots of my hands, I fell on my back. Then, I turned right to free my hands and that's when I felt that there was something in the pocket of my jeans.

I sat up straight and reached into the pocket of my jeans with my tied hands and felt a paper.

I took that out and I could sense that there was something written on it, only if I could open my eyes and see what was written.

I then put my brain to some use. The kind of paper in my hand was rough. Just like the paper the king used to write the notes.

The one to my surprise, and then I realized that there should be something in my pocket.

At first, I thought that it would help me escape from here; but then I realized that such a small thing would not let me kill the robots (if there were any) let alone help me escape.

But it was worth trying.

It took me almost five minutes to take the thing out of my pocket. I rolled it in my hands and realized that it was as long as my index finger. It was cylindrical in shape. When I found out that it was blunt from both sides, I gave up.

I mean, how could I cut ropes with something so small and blunt?

I kept it back in my pocket along with the paper and then put my back against the wall and that's when I realized that the ropes around my hands were metal. They were not ropes; it was solid metal!

I wished I was dead.

The thing that was covering my eyes was cloth. A thin cloth. I could open that with my hands.

I somehow managed to reach my hands to the cloth tied around my eyes, thanks to my long hands and extremely long fingers. I have a big hand.

Anyway, after a few minutes of struggle and an uncomfortable position; I managed to open the cloth around my eyes.

It took me a while to adjust my eyes to the darkness. When I looked around, I realized that I was really in a closet; except that there were no clothes or hangers. It was more like a room, a prison.

I looked around to spot a keyhole, a tiny one; through which only my fingers could fit.

I looked through it and for a moment I thought I was in Arrakis because a hot wind blew in my face at sand stinged my eyes. I fell back and tears came from my eyes.

There was some light coming from that small window-like thing. I decided to read what the message had said.

I searched my pocket and found that note again. It was in the small and beautiful writing of the king.

Dear Aiden,

We won't be able to interact for a while as I have to go a bit away from the kingdom for some secretive work.

I have one last gift for you. A gift that will help you in any situation. If you check your pocket, you will find a small gift. It's a weapon. It may seem harmless but it's really useful, especially when you are in trouble.

This thing is called a F13A Saber. Let me brief you on its functions. It can grow five feet long and be as short as your pinky finger if you wish. You can kill any robot using it if hit in the right place. It can burn anything to ashes when at full length. It can break metal, locker doors, or anything in its way. If it touches a robot, it'll burn to ashes.

It's a weapon that can react according to the situation you're in. Basically, it can read your mind; and according to that, it does what it needs to do in order to protect you.

Aiden, I'm afraid that people will try to harm you. So, don't trust anyone except me and Coco. Perhaps, not even me. There are possibilities that robots may try to make a clone of me and try to kill you.

I wondered why I didn't read this before, or why I hadn't realized that there was something in my pocket.

We'll make a code word, which only you and me know. The word is Colson. Don't share it with anyone. Make a code word with Coco as well. So, whenever we meet, ask me the code word, just to make sure it is me.

I can't write more as I'm undercover in a robot prison.

Try to find me as I can't escape on my own. There are several apes here with me. I can't tell you exactly where I am. The others might know. Free them and free me. We are in a desert.

I know I was there with you just five minutes ago, talking about my locket. Just after you went, I had to leave.

We encountered a few robots when I was dressed up as a soldier and I came here a bit earlier than I was supposed to. This message might have been kept while you were in the dressing room. Yes, just so that you know, your watch can stop time for two minutes.

One of the soldiers near you paused the time and kept this in your pocket. Good luck finding me Aiden. We all rely on you.

With best wishes,

Richards.

After reading that, I quickly took out the weapon from my pocket and concentrated all my power to make the weapon bigger.

After a few seconds of concentration, I opened my eyes to find a very big staff, blunt from both sides; much like bamboo except that it was made up of wood. *Wow, a wooden stick can break metal,* I thought in my mind.

I'm not a stick. Said a voice in my head which later realized that it was the F13A Saber speaking in my head.

Wow, now I'm speaking to a lifeless staff. I thought.

I will come in handy when you are in trouble. It spoke.

'Well; I am in trouble!'- I exclaimed.

Then, I noticed that the blunt staff had several markings etched on it; which suddenly began to glow in golden.

Then suddenly; a sharp edge was formed where it should have been blunt and then I knew exactly what to do.

After breaking some metal from my hands and legs, I took the staff (which had turned blunt again) and stood up, rubbing my legs and hands for some blood circulation.

I commanded the blunt staff to generate power to break the door. The etched markings grew golden again. I tightened my grip on the staff and advanced towards the metal door.

When the door and the staff met, there was a loud boom and so much power was generated from their contact that I fell backward and banged my back into the wall.

I coughed once or twice and rubbed my eyes as the wind blew sand into them. I ordered the staff to do something for my eyes as I couldn't fight with my eyes stinging with pain.

The explosion was so loud that I was sure that the robots must've heard it and were coming my way. So, it was best to get away from here as soon as possible.

But, of course; my life is never full of obstacles... and robots. Apes, the size of King Kong think I'm their savior.

Completely normal.

Just as I stepped out, I found almost twenty robots in my way.

Do something. Help me out. I thought.

On it boss. Just go with it. It spoke in my mind almost immediately.

Just go with what? I don't know how to fight. I'll die. I thought, now panicking.

But the staff didn't answer that question. All I knew was that I had to hit them right in the middle of the chest where the chip was there. If that was destroyed, the robot would be done for good.

Just then, the staff moved towards one of the robots, dragging me in the same direction. The staff hit the robot right in the middle of the chest and it evaporated into dust and mixed with the sand.

Then, I understood what it meant by 'just go with it.'

I let the staff take control of my body.

After taking one robot down, I turned towards the other robots confidently and matched my thoughts with the staff. When I did that, I felt a sudden energy flowing through my body and I felt that I was the most skilled and experienced fighter in the whole world.

I ran towards a robot and hit it right in the chest. Boom, it evaporated into dust. I turned around, dodged a punch, came behind the robot, and stabbed him in the chest. Dust.

I then narrowly missed a robot's laser attack, slid from between his legs, and... boom, ashes.

I then turned to two robots standing in a line and I knew exactly what to do. I advanced towards them and hit them right in the middle of the chest. The staff passed right through them; like a sharp knife cutting through cloth.

I held them up in mid-air before they evaporated into dust.

Before they evaporated into dust, I noticed something. I possibly couldn't have held robots in mid-air who were ten times my size. I then noticed that I was flying, holding the robots in mid-air.

'Woohoo!'- I yelled and the next one came and went by. After that, there was no time to pass. I was easily able to slash them apart like it was nothing.

After killing all the robots, I stopped levitating in mid-air and came down. Honestly speaking, with the staff, I felt like an overpowered hero of a movie. The golden light coming from the blunt staff stopped.

Once the light stopped glowing, I started to pant a bit and then I was back to my old form. I didn't feel like a skilled or experienced fighter, I felt like Aiden, the teenager Aiden.

At this point, I was relying on the staff completely to provide me with everything.

The voice of the staff spoke in my head, *What now boss?*

'Now,'- I said, 'We need to find the king.'

Amazing, said it's voice.

'Okay,'- I said. 'Now we need to get a view from above to spot any cells or prisons.' *Unless they are underground.* I added.

Don't think negatively boss, even if they are underground, we can; and we will find them. It spoke.

Excellent, so I had no privacy.

A golden light glowed from the staff and I started levitating in the air. Two feet... six feet... two kilometers *above* the ground (I know this because I asked the staff).

'Can we move a bit lower?'- I asked as I was feeling a bit dizzy at such a height.

This is the lowest I can go if you want to get a full view of the desert. It spoke in my head.

I sighed and looked around for any signs of prisons or any cells or anything that looked out of place in a desert.

I couldn't see anything except sand. I squinted my eyes but I still couldn't see anything and I didn't dare ask the staff to go higher.

So, do you want me to go a bit lower? It spoke. 'No, I want you to go around and check if there is anything that looks out of place in a desert.'- I groaned.

With that, we flew around for some minutes before I located some cells at a distance. I commanded the staff to speed up; but before it could reach the cell, it stopped abruptly.

What happened? Why did you stop? I thought.

There is an invisible force field here that does not allow me to go further. It was made by the robots to keep any outsider from coming in and any prisoner from escaping. This can only be deactivated by a robot. It spoke.

'Can you deactivate it?'- I asked.

Yes, I can but- It said.

'Then do it, what are we waiting for?'- I asked impatiently.

I can do it but I'm afraid that I won't be able to hold it for a long time. This force field has a lot of power. I will only be able to hold it for a few seconds. Two, to be precise. Don't feel discouraged sir, you can do it. Oh! I forgot to add one thing. After using such a large amount of power, I need at least one hour's rest to bring back my full power. It spoke.

Thank you, you gave me a piece of very helpful information. Very encouraging and not dangerous at all. I thought sarcastically.

You're welcome boss, and I think you are misunderstanding. This is very dangerous. It spoke.

Surely, wooden sticks don't understand sarcasm.

'Hey, what is the worst that can happen if you collide or touch this thing?'- I asked nervously.

The worst that can happen is that you die and burn to ashes or your body gets cut into tiny pieces. Pieces so tiny that it will be hard to find your pieces in the grains of sand. It spoke joyfully in my head.

Amazing. I thought and thankfully he didn't reply to that.

Okay, when I say 'now', you sprint forward as fast as you can. It spoke.

With that, we landed a bit closer to the force field and a golden light glowed from the staff. Then a voice yelled in my head which said, *NOW!*

I closed my eyes and ran straight for a few minutes and then I realized that nothing had happened to me. I then sighed with joy. I wondered what I would do without the staff.

I asked the staff, 'Can you navigate the fastest route for me that leads to the king?' No reply. I repeated my question twice before I realized that the staff needed an hour's rest before it could function again.

I concentrated with the staff in my hand. I asked it to be small again but when I opened my eyes, the staff was in the same form. I stared at it blankly for a few moments and then slammed my hand against my head. The staff would stay the same.

I looked around to look for any robots. Luckily, there were none. I wondered why there were no guards for the cells. Then I realized that someone may have informed the guards that I had escaped my prison. They then would have left the cells and would have come to get me. Without the staff; I was a little weakling and honestly, I was in no mood to fight any more robots.

I advanced towards the cells filled with apes looking for any king wearing a locket and a gold chain. Then I realized that the king may have worn the chain but not the locket as it would have given away that he was the king.

As far as I remember, there were at least thirty to forty holding cells and each one was filled with almost fifteen apes; but the last one, it was empty. I walked to one of the cells and asked one of the apes, 'Who was here?'

He said, 'I've heard about you. You are the messiah, right?'- he said in a scared voice as if they were afraid of me. 'Yes.'- I answered. 'I am the messiah.'

When I said that, I noticed that there was a sudden uplift in their mood. It was as though they had a hope that I would protect them, free them from here and I was not going to let them down.

I forgot all about the question I had asked them about the king and got busy in freeing the soldiers.

I took a look at the lock to see that there was no lock of any kind. There was just a tablet kind of thing attached to the bars of the prison. In the future; at least one thing did not change.

The prison bars.

'Do you have any idea how this could be opened?'- I asked. 'Yes, we need a robot for that.'- said one of the apes from the other cells. 'Now where do I get a robot from?'- I asked myself, frustrated.

'We have a robot head for a situation like this.'- said another ape from the cell I was trying to open. I couldn't believe my luck.

I impatiently looked at the robot head an ape was holding and asked him to give it to me, but then I realized that the head could not have passed from the gap between the prison bars.

I stamped my feet with exasperation. 'Is there any other way I can free you?'- I asked. 'Uhm... yes, there is another way.'- said one of the other apes. I looked at him with a sparkle of hope in my eyes. 'You need to break this.'- he said, pointing towards the tablet-like thing.

I leaned closer to the tablet to figure out any place I could hit to break it. I then noticed that there was a camera on the tablet, which I assumed would be for the face detection of the robots.

I took my staff and hit the tablet with the staff and to my surprise, it broke and the doors of the prison opened. The apes smiled at me and one of them even said thank you.

I went on to break the second prison when one of the freed apes said, 'I forgot to add that we don't have much time before the alarm goes off and the robots come here.'- he said. 'No,'- said another. 'The alarm has already alerted the robots. They must be coming this way.'- said the same ape. 'As far as I know, it should take at least ten minutes for the robots to reach here.'- said another.

'Let's not waste time. You, take the robot head and free the others. While for the rest of you, keep an eye out for the robots.'- I said commandingly.

One of the apes hurriedly took the robot's head and started to free the apes from the prison. Breaking the tablet was harder than the face-scanning thing. When I freed one of the cells, the other ape was already done with two and was moving on to the third.

Within two or three minutes, we were done freeing everyone. 'How many of you were held captive?'- I asked. 'Almost six hundred of us.'- said one after a small pause. I widened my eyes at the number. 'Okay, so this must be at least half the total army you have?'- I asked. 'Uhm... I guess this must be one-ninth or one-tenth of the whole army.'- said the one standing behind me.

I was still in shock and that's when one of the apes yelled, 'Robots are coming, get ready to attack. Soldiers, formation Z.'

With that, the apes started to run around and I thought that they were panicking as the robots were so close. I looked at the robots coming for a heartbeat and then back at the apes. To my surprise, all the apes were standing in a different position, and to me; it didn't look like any formation. But then, I realized what they were trying to do and it was genius.

Before they could charge toward the enemy, I shouted at the top of my lungs, 'Target the center of their chest as there is a chip there, which if destroyed will destroy them completely. But, if you hit anywhere else, they will regenerate.'

The apes nodded and the robots landed in front of us. As far as I remember, there were some hundred to two-hundred robots there.

The same ape who had yelled 'formation Z' shouted, 'Charge!'

With that, the first five lines charged at the robots. Ten lines were remaining. When the apes ran towards them, they were in a line, but when they reached a bit wider field of desert, they spread out in two horizontal lines. None of them had weapons and that's when I felt that I should enter the battlefield.

The robots looked as if they would easily overpower the apes. I realized that the ape who had shouted the commands at the soldiers was none other than the general of the army. An old enemy, the scarred ape.

I ran up to him, 'Hey, send more apes out there. They won't be able to survive.'- I said breathlessly. 'Yes, they won't survive.'- said the scarred ape calmly. 'Then send more apes there!'- I shouted, starting to lose my temper. 'Why?'- he asked me. 'Why?! You're asking me why, huh?!'- I said, losing my temper.

But according to the ape's expression, I decided not to talk and went and stood away from the ape.

After one or two seconds, I said, 'Then at least let me go out there.'- I shouted. 'No.'- he said normally but his voice reached me.

'Wonderful. Now we watch apes die.' I muttered angrily to myself.

XVI
ESCAPING THE PRISON

After breaking some metal from my hands and legs, I took the staff (which had turned blunt again) and stood up, rubbing my legs and hands for some blood circulation.

I commanded the blunt staff to generate power to break the door. The etched markings grew golden again. I tightened my grip on the staff and advanced towards the metal door.

When the door and the staff met, there was a loud boom and so much power was generated from their contact that I fell backwards and banged my back to the wall.

I coughed once or twice and rubbed my eyes as the wind blew sand into them. I ordered the staff to do something for my eyes as I couldn't fight with my eyes stinging with pain.

The explosion was so loud that I was sure that the robots must've heard it and were coming my way. So, it was best to get away from here as soon as possible.

But, of course; my life is never full of obstacles and robots, apes considering a teen their messiah. Completely normal.

Just as I stepped out, I found almost twenty robots in my way.

Do something. Help me out. I thought.

On it boss. Just go with it. It spoke in my mind almost immediately.

Just go with what? I don't know how to fight. I'll die. I thought, now panicking.

But the staff didn't answer that question. All I knew was that I had to hit them right in the middle of the chest where the chip was there. If that was destroyed, the robot would be done for good.

Just then, the staff moved towards one of the robots, dragging me in the same direction. The staff hit the robot right in the middle of the chest and it evaporated into dust and mixed with the sand.

Then, I understood what it meant by 'just go with it.'

I let the staff take control over my body.

After taking one robot down, I turned towards the other robots confidently and matched my thoughts with the staff. When I did that, I felt a sudden energy flowing through my body and I felt that I was the most skilled and experienced fighter in the whole world.

I ran towards a robot and hit it right in the chest. Boom, it evaporated into dust. I turned around, dodged a punch and came behind the robot and stabbed him in the chest. Dust.

I then narrowly missed a robot's laser attack, slid from between his legs and... boom, ashes.

I then turned to two robots standing in a line and I knew exactly what to do. I advanced towards them and hit them right in the middle of the chest. The staff passed right through them; like a sharp knife cutting through cloth.

I held them up in mid-air before they evaporated into dust.

Before they evaporated into dust, I noticed something. I possibly couldn't have held robots in mid-air who were ten times my size. I then noticed that I was flying, holding the robots in mid-air.

'Woohoo!'- I yelled and the next one came and went by. After that, there was no time-pass. I was easily able to slash them apart like it was nothing.

After killing all the robots, I stopped levitating in mid-air and came down. Honestly speaking, with the staff, I felt like an overpowered hero of a movie. The golden light coming from the blunt staff stopped.

Once the light stopped glowing, I started to pant a bit and then I was back to my old form. I didn't feel like a skilled or experienced fighter, I felt like Aiden, the teenager Aiden.

At this point, I was relying on the staff completely to provide me with everything.

The voice of the staff spoke in my head, *What now boss?*

'Now,'- I said, 'We need to find the king.'

Amazing, said it's voice.

'Okay,'- I said. 'Now we need to get a view from above to spot any cells or prison.' *Unless they are underground.* I added.

Don't think negatively boss, even if they are underground, we can; and we will find them. It spoke.

Excellent, so I had no privacy.

A golden light glowed from the staff and I started levitating in air. Two feet... six feet... two kilometers *above* the ground (I know this because I asked the staff).

'Can we move a bit lower?'- I asked as I was feeling a bit dizzy at such a height.

This is the lowest I can go if you want to get a full view of the desert. It spoke in my head.

I sighed and looked around for any signs of prisons or any cells or anything that looked out of pace in a desert.

I couldn't see anything except sands. I squinted my eyes but I still couldn't see anything and I didn't dare ask the staff to go higher.

So, do you want me to go a bit lower? It spoke. 'No, I want you to go around and check if there is anything that looks out of place in a desert.'- I groaned.

With that, we flew around for some minutes before I located some cells at a distance. I commanded the staff to speed up; but before it could reach the cell, it stopped abruptly.

What happened? Why did you stop? I thought.

There is an invisible force field here which does not allow me to go further. It was made by the robots to keep any outsider from coming in and any prisoner from escaping. This can only be deactivated by a robot. It spoke.

'Can you deactivate it?'- I asked.

Yes, I can but- It said.

'Then do it, what are we waiting for?'- I asked impatiently.

I can do it but I'm afraid that I won't be able to hold for a long time. This force field has a lot of power. I will only be able to hold it for a few seconds. Two, to be precise. Don't feel discouraged sir, you can do it. Oh! I forgot to add one thing. After using such a large amount of power, I need at least one hour's rest to bring back my full power. It spoke.

Thank you, you gave me a very helpful information. Very encouraging and not dangerous at all. I thought sarcastically.

Your welcome boss, and I think you are misunderstanding. This is very dangerous. It spoke.

Surely, staffs don't understand sarcasm.

'Hey, what is the worst that can happen if you collide or touch this thing?'- I asked it nervously.

The worse that can happen is that you die and burn to ashes or your body gets cut into tiny pieces. Pieces so tiny that it will be hard to find your pieces in the sand. It spoke joyfully in my head.

Amazing. I thought and thankfully he didn't reply to that.

Okay, when I say 'now', you sprint forward as fast as you can. It spoke.

With that, we landed a bit closer to the force field and a golden light glowed from the staff. Then a voice yelled in my head which said, *NOW!*

I closed my eyes and ran straight for a few minutes and then I realized that nothing had happened to me. I then sighed with joy. I wondered what I would to without the staff.

I asked the staff, 'Can you navigate the fastest route for me that leads to the king?' No reply. I repeated my question twice before I realized that the staff needed an hour's rest before it could function again.

I concentrated with the staff in my hand. I asked it to be small again but when I opened my eyes, the staff was in the same form. I stared at it blankly for a few moments and then slammed my hand against my head. The staff would stay the same.

I looked around to look for any robots. Luckily, there were none. I wondered why there were no guards for the cells. Then I realized that someone nay have informed the guards that I had escaped my prison. They then would have left the cells and would have come to get me. Without the staff; I was a little weakling and honestly, I was in no mood to fight any robots.

I advanced towards the cells filled with apes looking for any king wearing a locket and a gold chain. Then I realized that the king may have worn the chain but not the locket as it would have given away that he was the king.

As far as I remember, there were at least thirty to forty holding cells and each one was filled with almost fifteen apes; but the last one, it was empty. I asked who was here to one of the apes. He said, 'I've heard about you. You are the messiah, right?'- he said in a scared voice as if they were afraid of me. 'Yes.'- I answered. 'I am the messiah.'

When I said that, I noticed that there was a sudden uplift in their mood. It was as though they had a hope that I would protect them, free them from here and I was not going to let them down.

I forgot all about the question I had asked them about the king and got busy in freeing the soldiers.

I took a look at the lock to see that there was no lock of any kind. There was just a tablet kind of thing attached to the bars of the prison. In the future; at least one thing did not change. The prison bars.

'Do you have any idea on how this could be opened?'- I asked. 'Yes, we need a robot for that.'- said one of the apes from the other cells. 'Now where do I get a robot from?'- I asked myself, frustrated.

'We have a robot head for a situation like this.'- said another ape from the cell I was trying to open. I couldn't believe my luck.

I impatiently looked at the robot head an ape was holding and asked him to give it to me, but then I realized that the head could not have passed from the gap between the prison bars.

I stamped my feet with exasperation. 'Is there any other way I can free you?'- I asked. 'Uhm... yes, there is another way.'- said one of the other apes. I looked at him with a sparkle of hope in my eyes. 'You need to break this.'- he said, pointing towards the tablet like thing.

I leaned closer to the tablet to figure out any place I could hit to break it. I then noticed that there was a camera on the tablet, which I assumed that it would be for the detection of face of the robots.

I took my staff and hit the tablet with the staff and to my surprise, it broke and the doors of the prison opened. The apes smiled at me and one of them said thank you.

I went on to break the second prison when one of the freed apes said, 'I forgot to add that we don't have much time before the alarm goes off and the robots come here.'- he said. 'No,'- said another. 'The alarm as already alerted the robots. They must be coming this way.'- said the same ape. 'As far as I know, it should take at least ten minutes for the robots to reach here.'- said another.

'Let's not waste time. You, take the robot head and free the others. While for the rest of you, keep an eye out for the robots.'- I said commandingly.

One of the apes hurriedly took the robot head and started to free the apes out of the prison. Breaking the tablet was harder than the face scanning thing. When I freed one of the cells, the other ape was already done with two and was moving on to the third.

Within two or three minutes, we were done freeing everyone. 'How many of you were held captive?'- I asked. 'Almost six-hundred of us.'- said one after a small pause. I widened my eyes at the number. 'Okay, so this must be at least half the total army you have?'- I asked. 'Uhm... I guess this must be one-ninth or one-tenth of the whole army.'- said the one standing behind me.

I was still in shock and that's when one of the apes yelled, 'Robots are coming, get ready to attack. Soldiers, formation Z.'

With that, the apes started to run around and I thought that they were panicking as the robots were so close. I looked at the robots coming for a heartbeat and then back at the apes. To my surprise, all the apes were standing in a different position, and to me; it didn't look like any formation. But then, I realized what they were trying to do and it was genius.

Before they could charge towards the enemy, I shouted at the top of my lungs, 'Target the center of their chest as there is a chip there, which if destroyed will destroy them completely. But, if you hit anywhere else, they will regenerate.'

The apes nodded and the robots landed in front of us. As far as I remember, there were some hundred to two-hundred robots there.

The same ape who had yelled 'formation Z' shouted, 'Charge!'

With that, the first five lines charged at the robots. Ten lines were remaining. When the apes ran towards them, they were in a line, but when they reached a bit wider field of desert, they spread out in two horizontal lines. None of them had weapons and that's when I felt that I should enter the battlefield.

The robots looked as if they would easily overpower the apes. I realized that the ape who had shouted the commands at the soldiers was none other than the general of the army. An old enemy, the scarred ape.

I ran up to him, 'Hey, send more apes out there. They won't be able to survive.'- I said breathlessly. 'Yes, they won't survive.'- said the scarred ape calmly. 'Then send more apes there!'- I shouted, starting to lose my temper. 'Why?'- he asked me. 'Why?! You're asking me why, huh?!'- I said, losing my temper.

But according to the ape's expression, I decided not to talk and went and stood away from the ape.

After one or two seconds, I said, 'Then at least let me go out there.'- I shouted. 'No.'- he said normally but his voice reached me.

'Wonderful. Now we watch apes die.' I muttered angrily to myself.

XVII
I GET HIT BY LASER

The robots and the apes charged towards each other, enthusiastically ready to finish each other.

But then, the second line moved backward, and the first bent down on their knees. I didn't know what they were doing and was not at all interested in seeing them die while I was just sitting there and staring at them. That's what a messiah would do, sit around and watch people dying.

The first line lowered their heads and the second line came running towards them. I straightened up my back when I realized what they were going to do.

The second line took the help of the first line and jumped and launched themselves into the air. Together, with amazing synchronization, they punched right into the center of the chest of the robot, and some forty soldiers evaporated into dust in front of my eyes.

Then, the second line bent down and the first line went over them. Again, with the amazing power and synchronization of the apes, another forty robots evaporated into dust. So, out of one hundred twenty robots, eighty were already evaporated to dust.

After that, the robots realized what was happening and changed their positions. They surrounded the apes. I called out to the scarred ape and told him to send more soldiers, but he just wouldn't listen.

Instead, he told me that he knew that the apes wouldn't survive, and he wouldn't risk the lives of other apes to save them.

When he said that, I got so angry and frustrated that I wanted to fire that scarred ape from his job. Unfortunately, only the king had that kind of authority. So what? I was on a greater post than the king, I could do anything I wanted.

But; I caught a hold of my emotions and in that state of mind, I could only think of one thing to do; and that is what I did.

I took my powerless blunt staff and advanced into the battlefield. I knew I wouldn't be much of a use without my powerful staff. But at that point in time, I was ready to give my life for the apes and I could do anything just to protect them.

I ran towards one of the robots and backstabbed it. To my surprise, it evaporated into dust. So, the staff *was* useful; with or without power. The only thing was that it didn't go through as smoothly as it did before. I needed to apply a bit of force so that it could go through the robot and come out.

Seeing me, the other apes got encouraged and hit the robots in front of them, evaporating them into dust.

Another wave of robots came and went by. I killed some seven or eight robots (I can't believe I still remember the number!).

Unfortunately, the ninth robot that I went to kill hit me with the laser thing. It just touched my cheekbone and the next moment, a thin line of blood appeared there. Then it started to bleed.

I got so angry at him, that I just ran towards him and was about to stab him when I felt a stinging pain right in the center of my stomach.

When I looked down at my stomach, I saw that the red laser was there. I looked behind to see that the laser had passed right through my body.

After a few seconds, a red bloodstain started to form on my perfectly white T-shirt. I dropped my stick and put both my hands on my stomach to prevent blood loss. But unfortunately, I had already lost a lot of blood.

I dropped down on my knees and fell down with my stomach flat. The next thing I know is that my vision is going blurry and I can hear some faint footsteps of apes around me, charging at the robot who had made me fall to the ground.

I thought I was dying and there was no coming back. But... honestly, I don't believe I'm saying this. As I was the messiah and a so-called protector, I couldn't die so easily. I mean seriously, name me a single movie or a book where the main hero of the book/movie dies and the book/movie keeps going on.

Got none, right?

Same for this book. I don't die. Which I wanted to at this point.

☙

When I woke up, I found myself in a bed with a bad-smelling green ointment on my face and stomach.

I couldn't sit up straight because of the pain in my stomach. I wondered whether the laser thing had gone through my bones as well. I decided not to think about it.

At this point, I didn't know how many more times I had to die and come back to life. Honestly, I would be happier if I dyed.

Anyway, I looked up at the ceiling and it didn't look like I was in the palace. When I thought of the palace, I realized that I had forgotten all about the king. I still needed to rescue him.

I looked sideways and realized that I was in a tent. As the wind blew, I noticed the sand outside and realized that I was still in the desert.

I sighed; as it now would be easier for me to find the king. I was certain that the king was somewhere near me. 'Someone there?'- I asked.

An ape peeked through the door and shouted, 'He's awake! He's awake!' Two more apes then came inside the tent.

Once they all had settled down, I asked 'For how long had I passed out?' and panted heavily. I was shocked that I started to sweat by only saying a few words. I wondered if that was because of the heat or my weakness and blood loss.

'It's almost been an hour since you passed out.'- said the ape standing to the left. 'No, it's been one hour and twenty-three minutes; to be precise.'- said the ape standing to the right.

'Thanks for the information, guys. Uhm... are you the only ones here or are there more?'- I asked them and then winced in pain. 'There are only three of us here.'- the one in the middle replied.

I nodded and asked again, 'Then where are the others?' 'They've gone to rescue the king.'- replied the one on the left again.

'Are they with the General?'- I asked almost immediately. They nodded. 'He's such a bad General.'- I said. 'Sorry messiah, but the soldiers are called the general and the head of the army is called the lieutenant.'- said the ape standing in the center. 'Wait a moment, isn't lieutenant the lowest rank in the army?'- I asked. 'No.'- they replied.

I then realized that things might be a bit different in the future. 'Wait a second, aren't you guys the ones who the lieutenant sent to fight the robots?'- I noticed. They silently nodded once again. 'You did an amazing job out there.'- I said cheerfully.

They smiled and said, 'Thank you.'

I looked up again to the ceiling and moved my legs and that's when I noticed that there was something near my leg. I strained my neck a bit and looked at that thing. It was my staff. That brought me back to why I was here. That brought my senses back.

My smile vanished from my face. I looked at the last ape who was going to exit. 'Wait.'- I said and he turned around to look at me. 'Out of a hundred, how many chances are there that I will come back unharmed and will bring the king into safety if I go to the battlefield in this condition.'

'Sorry to say but there is less than one percent chance that you will be victorious. In fact, there is not even a single percent chance that you will be able to walk properly much less lead the army into battle.'- said the ape.

Hearing the conversation, the other apes also came back into the tent. I grunted angrily and tried to keep my voice as calm as possible, 'Where is the king? Do you know where he is?'- I asked. They nodded. 'How big was the head start they received?'- I asked. 'Almost an hour.'- said the ape to the left.

I clenched my fist and hit the bed angrily. Although I knew that I wouldn't be much of a use in the war. I knew that the lieutenant would be ready to kill soldiers if necessary and would not even send reinforcements.

'So, you know where the king is, right? Take me there.'- I said. 'But you're in no fit condition to--'

'I know I'm not ready, but I can't let other apes die because of him.'- I said, trying to keep my cool; but that was hard as it was really hot outside and the sweat kept tickling me. To top that off, they'd gotten a head start.

'Got a camel?'- I asked.

XVIII

THE KING, A GLADIATOR

I took my staff and used it like a walking stick as my legs were wobbly and because of the heat, I was feeling even worse. I wondered why the king had said that it was going to snow.

The apes helped me get on the camel and we started our journey. When it had been some five minutes after we left the tent, I realized that the staff would be back with its annoying thoughts. Honestly saying, having another voice speaking in your head which is not yours is hectic.

Knock, Knock, anyone there, trespassing my mind? I thought.

Yes boss? I am fully recovered now. Order me to do anything. Said a familiar voice in my head.

I smiled and thought, *can you recover me from this injury?*

I'm not sure but I can try. Allow me to inspect your injuries. It spoke.

Then, I had a ticklish feeling near my wounds, which was urging me to scratch it but I only knew that it would hurt me more.

I can heal these injuries a bit only so that you can fight. But, if you exhaust yourself too much, then the wounds would open again and you won't be able to walk. It spoke in my head.

Okay, do anything, just heal these. In fact, the wound on my face is okay, just heal the wound on my stomach. Anyways, how long will it take to heal my wound? I thought.

Uhm... I think it will take an hour to repair. But, remember, if anything even touches you on your wound, it will open again and if-

Yeah, yeah, I know. Just heal it quickly. I thought, interrupting it.

After some more fifteen minutes of tolerating the heat, I asked, 'How much longer?' 'It's only some twenty to twenty-five kilometres from here.'- said one of the apes. I gave a disappointed sigh and asked, 'Okay, how much more time will it take us to reach there?' 'Judging by the heat and the camel's speed, I think it will take us at least half an hour or forty-five minutes to reach there.'- said one of the other apes.

I asked the staff, *is their any other way which will lead us faster?*

I know only one way, if only you agree to it. It spoke in my head almost immediately.

Tell me, I am ready to do anything to reach there. I said impatiently.

We can fly there. It suggested. *Nice idea but there's only one problem. We both can fly there, bur these three can't; and I don't want to leave them here.* I thought.

They can come too. There's something in your jeans pocket. Give it to them and they can come along. It spoke in my head.

I searched my pocket and found three very weird looking things. It was stones, black obsidian. It was very small in shape. Although it was a lot bigger than my palm, it still looked a trivial thing. It had the same markings etched on it like the staff, except that it was a lot smaller.

I explained to them to hold it tightly in their hands and concentrate on that stone in their hands. The next moment, we were flying above the dunes at a speed of two-hundred kilometres per hour.

So, how much time will it take us to reach our destination? I thought.

It would take us exactly seven and a half minutes to reach our destination. Its voice spoke in my head.

***

When we landed, I saw that the apes hadn't reached there yet and I was thankful for that as I couldn't bear seeing apes die.

We got a bit closer and I saw what was happening. I clenched my fists and wanted to run and kill all the four robots, including the thousand others.

Okay, so let me give a very vivid description of the scene in front of my eyes. The king was in an arena, surrounded by four robots in four directions. The king was fighting as a gladiator, for the entertainment of the other robots.

I knew it was like knocking on death's door if I walked into the arena. I knew I could kill the ones in the arena. But the ones surrounding them, maybe not. Certainly not.

Hey, will laser destroy the robots? I thought, an idea forming in my mind.

Yes. It spoke in my head.

Can you produce laser out of your blunt sides by any chance? I thought.

Yes, I can but why- OH, I see why you're asking this. Nice idea. It spoke in my head, appreciating my idea. *So, you wanna do it now or...*

Now. I thought.

Okay, laser in three...two...one... It spoke.

Golden light glowed from etched markings on the wooden stick and I pointed towards one of the robots surrounding the king. I targeted right in the center of its chest and the moment it touched the robot, it evaporated into dust.

Even the king looked surprised at the sudden vanishing of the robot. Then, when he spotted the laser, he realized what was happening and immediately looked at me and smiled. I smiled back and winked at him.

The other two soldiers advanced towards the king but the king dodged one and I evaporated the other into dust. My next question to the staff was, *can the stones do it too?*

When the stone in their hands started to glow golden, they looked at me and I nodded. Thankfully, they understood what to do and started evaporating the other robots into dust.

I didn't know why, but the robots didn't attack us, even when the direction of the laser was clear. I had a feeling that this could be a trap.

Anyways, long story short, we evaporated all the robots before the apes came and rescued the king.

Okay, if you want to know some details, I can give you some of the epic things that happened.

Okay so while we were evaporating them into dust, I thought a mosquito bit me on my neck and I turned back to kill it with the laser.

But, to my surprise, I evaporated a robot into dust which was about to kill me and was inches from me, literally inches. The three apes beside me thought that I had excellent reaction and hearing sense. But actually, it was mere luck.

Okay, I saw one of the robots coming towards the king as he ran towards us and I put my laser on him. Actually, there were some seven or eight robots standing in a line, which evaporated into dust one by one. It was so cool.

Honestly, at this point, I was feeling that I was actually in a video game, killing robots as if I had some spy mission to protect the hostage: the king.

I was having so much fun that I wanted to become a rabbit and jump around. You know those times when you get super excited and you don't know what to do or how to express your feelings.

Then, out of nowhere. The ground started to move, like an earthquake was about to happen. (If you've seen dune, only then you will understand the next part). Sorry, I'm a bit too obsessed with the movie.

So, when the king came to us and we started to head back, the ground started moving and we all looked back. It was as if a sandworm was about to come out. For those of you who don't know how a sandworm comes out of sand, let me tell you. So, if you take an hourglass and flip it, the sand in it comes down (obviously). If you take a look from the top, the sand first goes down from the middle and then from the sides. It's much like that. Sandworms appear like that.

Ok, I was almost expecting one to come out and gobble us all up. Fortunately, there was no sandworm. Instead, there was a massive robot. Ten times bigger than the normal robots. I hardly came up till his ankle.

I knew we couldn't fight it so I asked the staff to make a protective shield around us and fly us to the tent where we will be at a safe distance from the giant robot. I mean, it felt kind of insignificant to use the term 'giant' for a massive robot as the regular-sized robots seemed like toys in front of him and to me, I felt that I would look like a dot. Wait a second, not even a dot, a molecule in air or even an atom.

I knew that we'd escaped the massive robot for now but I was certain that we will have to face this massive robot in the final battle and I couldn't form a shield around all the apes.

I had a feeling that the final battle was going to be a deathmatch. It was either us or them. We couldn't have a single weakness. For that, first of all, I needed to tell the king to fire the lieutenant/general.

Wait, you can't fire a person from the forces. But we can surely give him a lower post and make someone more capable the general.

XIX

I VISIT THE ARMOURY

Long story short, we flew to the palace, which was a long ride. Actually, when we were flying over to the tent in the desert, we met the rest of the army midway and told them to return as the king was safe.

We had to wait near the tent for almost thirty minutes for the army.

The staff could only carry one hundred fifty apes at once. I was not counted, so we carried one extra.

The distance between the desert and the palace was some three hundred kilometers. Thanks to the staff's speed, we reached there in ten to fifteen minutes.

When we reached there, I realized the complete ground was covered with snow. I didn't know how deep the snow was, I didn't want to know. I just prayed to God, hoping the snow wouldn't be deep enough to engulf me.

The staff kept me hovering a few millimeters above the snow while it covered three-fourths of the legs of apes.

After reaching the palace safe and sound, I told the staff to bring the others as well. After some three or four rounds, everyone was there.

When the soldiers who had come with us left, the first thing I asked the king was, 'Can you fire the Gene- lieutenant?'

The king looked surprised by the sudden question. 'Uhm... I, No. I can't fire the lieutenant from the army, but I can certainly give him a lower post of a general. But why do you ask so?'- asked the king. 'During a fight between the robots and apes, that guy asked the soldiers to do formation Z and when the soldiers got surrounded by robots, he said that he was not going to send any other apes as he could not risk the lives of other apes to save eighty. I mean, if it was two or three, it was still understandable. But eighty?'- I said.

The king nodded lightly but didn't reply. I guess he also wanted to remove the ape from his position and give someone worthy of the position of lieutenant. Sorry, but how can a general be a smaller post than a lieutenant? It's hilarious. I can't stop laughing at this.

So, the king then guided me to a place filled with weapons. It was the armory. I stopped on the doorstep, admiring the weapons.

If you're wondering whether the armory would be loaded with spears and shields and stuff, you're wrong. Oh, wait, you're partially right. It was spears and shields until the king showed me what it really was.

The whole armory was loaded with watches. Not the Tommy Hilfiger ones, plain and old looking, second-handed. But I noticed that it had a protective layer around it as if it were very precious.

The ceiling was high and I felt a bit warm inside the armoury. It was as if a heater was in there, but I didn't spot any.

The king put his hand on a random place on the layer and a tablet appeared on the place where his hand was. He then entered a fifteen-digit code and deactivated the shield.

He took out one watch and said, 'Come in Aiden. What are you doing out there?'

When he said that, I then realized that I was still standing at the doorstep of the armory. I closed my open mouth and came in.

The king told me to stay a few steps away from him. 'I'm going to show you how to fight with this.'

'Hang on a minute, tell me the code.'- I asked as this could be a very good opportunity for a robot to kill me as I didn't have my staff and there was no one around, and even if they managed to reach here, the robot would have killed me and gone.

'Colson.'- replied the king.

I nodded but I was sure to maintain distance. The king pressed a non-existent button in a normal analog watch.

When he touched the button, it turned into a spear with etched markings on it, similar to my staff. I opened my mouth to speak but as if the king read my mind, he said, 'Yes Aiden, this is powered when the F13A Saber is around. If this even touches a robot, it will kill it. Even if it's not in the middle of its chest.' and smiled at me.

Then the king double-tapped the same button and the spear turned into a shield with the same etched markings of my staff.

'This object can absorb and bounce back any energy directed at it. So, when someone hits it with force, it rebounds that force right back at them, knocking them down in the process.'- he said.

Just then, the shield glowed a dim yellow light from it. The king noticed it and said, 'I think that the Saber came back. You can go collect it.' and I left the armory.

Once I had taken my staff, I noticed that the king was not far behind. When he came close enough, I said, 'If you had such cool weapons, then why didn't you use them during the first war?'- I asked. 'First war?! You were there during the first was? That was some ages ago. It was some ten thousand years back if I remember correctly.'- he said. 'No, I mean the latest war.'- I said. 'Oh.'- he said, still looking surprised.

'Oh, actually, we- you know that we have a secret lab, right? Coco must've told you about it,' he said. I nodded and he continued, 'We were told that these would be ready before the war. But; unfortunately, the robots attacked two days before from when our scientists had predicted and so, we had to go into battle unprepared. Luckily, we won that battle. This time, we're determined to finish the robots once and for all.'- he said.

'What are you going to do when you win the war? I mean, you will just rule the whole kingdom yourself. There'll be no adventures, you'll get bored.'- I said.

The king laughed and said, 'Our scientists are saying that there is a massive asteroid coming our way. Similar to the Chicxulub impactor. We are planning to make a force field big enough to protect the whole earth.' and smiled. 'We have a lot of work to do, kiddo.'- he said.

I didn't know what I could reply to that so I just nodded.

'Uhm... is this all, or are there more weapons?'- I asked. 'Of course, we have more weapons. But that is not our priority. First, I must explain all the formations used on the battlefield to you.'- he said.

After two or three minutes of walk, we reached a room where several maps and blueprint designs of the palace covered the walls of the room. There were several papers scattered across the table which was located in the middle of the room.

This room had no kind of protective shields around it. The papers on the walls were yellow with age and the edges were torn for most. I thought it was made by a machine until I looked closely and realized that it was hand-drawn.

There are exactly twenty-three battle formations. Don't worry, I won't go into the details of the formations. I'll save you that pain. It's a long list and is very complicated.

After explaining the various formations to me, he showed me the blueprint of the castle and explained every part of it (I didn't see how that could help in the war).

He told me that we had some thirty thousand to thirty-five thousand soldiers. We had twenty missiles, one hundred and fifty archers, fifty cannons, and two hundred apes with guns.

I was sure that we couldn't lose with that kind of army. 'Okay, beyond this, is there any other thing I should know about?'- I asked. The king thought for a while and said, 'Right now, I don't remember. If I remember anything else you need to know, I will inform you.'- he said.

We shortly left the room. I offered to drop him to his room and he agreed. 'Do you have any reports or any information on when the robots might attack?'- I asked after a few minutes.

'No, the robots might attack anytime now.'- he said.

'Then what are we waiting for? Change the lieutenant immediately and tell the soldiers to take the weapons and stay alert at all times.'- I said.

'There's a big ceremony for the change of the lieutenant in the palace.'- he said. 'Then I guess we'll need to skip that part.'- I said immediately which I then realized sounded a bit rude.

'Okay, we both can go together to announce that we have a new lieutenant in the army and to stay alert. Once they take the weapons, I will send soldiers to different parts of our palace to protect it.'- I said and we both turned toward the place where the soldiers were relaxing.

Much to my surprise, all the soldiers were sitting right outside the palace, and by all, I mean all. Thousands of them were sitting near a fireplace. They were having fun, chilling near the warm fireplace, laughing and sharing jokes with each other, enjoying a warm drink cupped in their hands, it was like that they were having the time of their lives. I so wanted to join them that I almost asked the king if I could do so. But then I controlled myself and set my priorities.

I looked at the king and we shared the same expression that said, *they're having fun. Let them have it while they still can as we don't know how many will die in the war. But right now, it's urgent. We can't get emotional right now.*

We both went out and the soldiers looked quite alarmed. Some of them looked so alarmed that they almost dropped their drink.

'Me and the messiah have decided that Caleb Anderson will no longer be the lieutenant.'- said the king in a loud voice. I could make out that there were several smiling faces across the area, and the ones who were not smiling were trying to keep a straight face. The only one who was not looking happy was Caleb Anderson aka the scarred ape (no hate). My sworn enemy.

'So, I want to make someone else, who is more worthy to become the lieutenant of the army. The new lieutenant is...' he paused and shouted, 'Edward Matthew!'

When the king said this name, apes couldn't help but dance around and be overjoyed. They couldn't express their feelings. At that point, only two apes didn't celebrate, one was Caleb; who was in extreme pain and the other one was who I expected it to be Edward; who was shocked and was still wondering if this was a dream.

I wanted to go and congratulate Edward but the snow would engulf me. Just then, my staff came to me and helped me pass the snow.

I made my way through the overjoyed apes and stopped next to Edward. 'You must be Edward.'- I said, trying to keep my voice as formal, patient, and not like a teenager, but like a messiah.

'Y-Yes, I am Edward.'- he said, breaking out of his shock. I couldn't contain myself and hugged him although my hands didn't even reach his back.

'Congratulations Edward. After all, I guess I was not the only one who wanted that ape to get removed from that position.'- I said. He smiled at me and I smiled back. 'Good luck Edward.' I said and patted him gently on the back.

Once I reached the king's side, he cleared his throat and brought all the attention back to him. Once the laughing had died out completely, he said, 'And as for Caleb, he will be assigned the post of a general. I'm sorry Edward but we don't have time for celebrations. We'll make sure we do it after the war ends.'

I saw the fear and nervousness they faced at the end of the sentence. I knew that they were wondering if they would survive the war to have a party.

'Hey, why are you all so sad, huh? Edward, you have a bonus after the war ends. We'll be celebrating you being the new lieutenant and we'll also be celebrating our victory; and don't you worry, they don't call me messiah for nothing. I and my staff will protect you. No one will die. I promise, and trust me; I never break a promise. So, cheer up buddies!'- I said enthusiastically and thankfully the mood lifted.

'Okay, finish up your drink and then take the weapons from the armory. We never know when the robots might attack. I don't want any apes to die without fighting.'- said the king. 'The armory is opened. Go and get the weapons.'- he said and we both started to walk to the gates.

When the king had gone in, I turned back, gave them a thumbs up, and winked at them. In return, they all raised their cups in the air and I hurried to keep up with the king before he noticed my absence.

'Uhm... is there any way we can contact? You know, just in case of an emergency.'- I said. 'Yes.'- he said and handed me over a pair of wireless earphones.

I must have looked surprised as he handed me over wireless earphones and said, 'So, these are called earphones—'

'I know what earphones are, they were used in our time as well.'- I interrupted. 'Uhm... okay, then you must know how to use them.'- he said. I nodded and after a few seconds of awkward silence, he left for his room and I left for mine.

XX

I EXPLORE A SECRET BELOW THE BATHROOM

Once I was in my room, I took out my socks and combat boots and put my staff near my boots.

It was when I laid down on my bed, I realized now tired I was and how badly my body was aching.

I put my legs inside the warm blanket and turned my back to the window wall. I then realized that there was a weird symbol etched on the wall next to the bathroom door.

I was inquisitive to go and look at what it was but I was feeling sleepy and very lazy to take out my legs from the warm blanket, but what if it was a secret bunker, or the secret lab Coco was talking about.

I got up from my bed and I couldn't help shiver. I went to the wall and saw how detailed it was. I then noticed that there was a circle in the middle with complicated designs and a few centimetres thick vertical lines on both the sides.

I took me a moment to realize what it was. I ran to my staff and placed the one of the blunt edges on the circle in the middle.

It fit perfectly. First, the etched markings glowed golden and that's when I heard some mechanical whirring and for a moment, I thought that the robots broke into my room.

Fortunately, the mechanical whirring was something else.

The sky-blue circular mat placed next to the bathroom moved towards the side on its own to reveal a secret passage. I wondered why this was not included in the palace's blueprint.

There was a ladder going down till I couldn't see it. It was completely dark inside.

I removed my staff from the wall and it produced enough golden light for me to use it as a torch in the dark.

Without hesitation, I started to climb down from the ladder. I asked the staff to hover near me as I couldn't climb down while holding it.

After a few minutes of climbing down, I reached the ground. The moment my bare feet touched the ground, a blinding light flashed right in my eyes, causing me to cover them.

I adjusted my eyes to the bright light and to my surprise, it was a room bigger than mine. It was so big that it could fit ninety-hundred elephants easily and there would still be plenty of space left for two massive robots to fit.

It had a large number of weapons like bows and arrows, the watches the king showed me, rope darts, swords, laser guns, rifles and several more which I was seeing for the first time. I guess they were some very advanced weapons.

I walked across the room and spotted a fridge. When I opened it, I found that there was a lot of frozen meat, curd and a lot of other stuff. You could use that in case of a zombie apocalypse. I could survive on that for a year or two at least.

I looked around and spotted some medicines, whose names I didn't bother to read. There were tablets and the liquid medicines and some bad green smelling liquid that the apes had put on my wounds during our time in the desert.

In short, it was a bunker.

After taking a look at all that, I started to climb the stairs back up. The moment my feet lifted off the ground, it was dark again.

After a few minutes, I was back up with my staff and I put the bathroom mat on the place from where I had climbed. I heard mechanical whirring for a few seconds and then it stopped.

I placed my staff next to my bed when I got my legs back into the warmth of the blanket. My body relaxed and I looked at the view outside the window. I took out my denim jacket and placed it beside me. It was then when I noticed that the bloodstain on my white t-shirt was gone.

Thanks Staff, for healing me and removing the bloodstain. I thought sleepily.

It was my duty to do so, boss. It spoke in my mind.

I smiled to myself and closed my eyes, drifting into the world of dreams.

***

When I woke up, I was still half asleep, woken up by a weird buzzing sound which I thought to be a mosquito. I turned around and found my staff glowing dangerously. I thought it was trying to tell me something.

Boss, this thing is buzzing continuously. I tried to shut it down, but nothing happened. It spoke in my head.

I saw that the case of the earphone was vibrating. That must be some improvements they made because as far as I knew, earphone cases didn't vibrate.

I opened the case and put on the earphone.

For a moment, there was no noise from that side, just some panicked voices and heavy breathing and shouting, there was also some screeching sounds.

'Hello?'- I said. 'Hello, is anyone there?'- I asked, a bit loudly. 'Aiden, Aiden, is that you?'- said the king in a panicked voice. 'Yes, it's me. Is everything okay there?'- I asked, trying to keep my voice calm.

'Come down Aiden, quickly. We don't have much time.'- he said in a panicked voice. 'Why, what happened?'- I asked, sitting up straight

and rubbing my sleepy eyes.
    'We've been attacked.'

XXI

I KILL A MASSIVE ROBOT

I didn't need an invitation to come and join the battle.

I threw my blanket aside and took my staff, wore my combat boots and ran towards the entrance.

The army of the apes was huge, but in front of their army, our seemed trivial; and to top that of, they had two massive robots. We were so dead.

Still, I took the lead and concentrated hard on my staff and then hit it on the ground. A power radiated from my staff and powered all the other weapons. A golden light passed through all the weapons.

I then noticed that the robots stopped at a distance and weren't coming closer. Some of them just evaporated by themselves. When I looked closely, I saw that there was a protective force field protecting the palace.

I had admiration for whatever or whoever was holding that. I was feeling nervous, worried whether we would survive or not. I turned around and I could feel the fear in their hearts and minds.

If I looked scared, we wouldn't have a chance against them. I knew they had noticed how big the army was.

I shouted, 'Force field down.' and thankfully, they heard me and we charged at each other.

I had to see my mother. What would happen to her if I died? Everybody had their hopes on me to protect them. I couldn't let them down.

I shouted angrily and ran at my full speed. I reduced one or two robots to dust just when my staff touched them. I didn't need to target them in the middle of the chest.

I fought and made my way through the robots towards the massive one. While fighting my way through them, I lost count.

Honestly, no robot attacked me while I fought my way through them.

When I reached it, I realized that I was hardly the size of his little finger.

Staff, I need you to help me fly up there to his chest. I thought.

I'm afraid I can't do that because I'm powering all the apes' weapons. If I help you fly up there, I can't give full power to the weapons and our army will weaken a little; giving the robots a golden opportunity to kill the apes easily. It will take a lot of power for me to give full strength to all of them and help you fly there as well. As a result, I will power down in the battle and will weaken the whole army and if-

Shut up. Don't give me such a long explanation. I didn't ask you to read out the Wikipedia. Just tell me if there's any other way to go up there. I thought angrily, slashing robots while thinking.

By climbing. It spoke bluntly. I had clearly hit a nerve.

Thank you. I thought back bitterly.

I cleared the path off robots and took a few steps back and ran towards the massive robot, nailing the highest jump I could ever have done (most probably because the staff helped me do so).

I caught hold of the massive robot's leg. I started to slip.

I struggled to hold the robot's leg. Just then, with my full power, I pierced the staff through its leg and made a whole there, making the wires inside's it's leg clearly visible.

I put my feet where I had stabbed him and continued my journey like that. I realized that when my Saber came in contact with the robot, it didn't evaporate, that meant I had to go all the way up to the chip to kill it.

I saw how close the robot had come to the palace. I hurried up to his chest, stabbing on his legs.

While doing this, I wondered why I was doing all this. Why was I helping the apes. Had I grown some feelings for them? Did I start to like them? No, I couldn't have developed likings for the apes. I mean, they were my friends, but why was I risking my life for them? They surely weren't that important to me. I told myself that I wasn't fighting for them, I was fighting for my mother. Why was I figthing for my mother?

I turned around to see that he was even closer to the palace now and I had not even crossed its legs.

Hey buddy, can you make my jumps longer? I thought.

When the staff didn't reply, I thought that he hadn't heard me and I didn't have the time to repeat it.

I took another jump and noticed that I had covered a bit more distance than I did before.

I knew that the staff had heard me.

When I made it up to the chest, I noticed that the place where the chip was supposed to be was made of glass. I could honestly see the chip there, glowing a dangerous red.

I made two dents for my legs and made myself comfortable there. I gripped my staff tightly with both my hands and channelled all my power to my hands.

I hit the staff to the glass, only to make a crack.

I held the staff again and channelled all my power to my hands once again.

But, before I could hit the glass once again to shatter it into pieces, my legs slipped from the dents I had made, as though an invisible force was pulling me backwards.

I didn't panic because I knew the staff would save me. I closed my eyes and concentrated on my staff. But then I noticed that I wasn't falling down. I was never falling down.

I looked at the robot's chest to see that my staff was placed firmly right at the center of the robot's chest.

Too bad the robot had noticed that something was trying to destroy it. The robot had held my denim jacket in his fingers and was moving it rapidly, causing me to fall a bit down every time. I struggled to hold the denim jacket. If I moved, I would fall a bit more.

I knew that I couldn't do anything except falling down. I knew that if I wanted to escape, I had to fall down. I let go of the denim jacket, falling down with full speed. Wind roared in my ears drowning the sound of chaos around me. Closing my eyes, I steadied my breathing and slowed my rapidly beating heart. I knew that I would fall touch the ground any moment and I didn't dare look down. Concentrating and slowing my breathing, I unclenched the fist of my right hand, removing all the negative things into the trash bin.

As expected, my stick flew towards my hand and I held it tightly. Together, for one last time, we hit the glass and it shattered into pieces.

I got inside before the robot could get hold of me again. I smashed the chip into pieces and just as I started to celebrate my victory, I realized one thing.

The head had started to evaporate into dust. I hadn't thought about that.

Till the time I realized what to do, the robot had completely evaporated into dust and I was falling down at full speed.

The staff helped me land down swiftly and I ran towards the king, killing robots on the way.

Once I reached him, I realized that he was using a rope dart. I couldn't help but admire how swiftly and easily he was killing them.

The king noticed me and said, 'What are you doing here?' but kept killing the robots.

'Can I have one like that too?'- I asked, killing robots, walking beside the king.

Then, out of nowhere, he produced a rope dart and gave it to me.

Then I realized that I didn't know how to use it. Then, I said what I had actually come to say to the king, 'Can you ask the archers or the snipers to hit the massive robot.'

'I have already told them that. They're working on it.'- he said and for the first time after the court incident; the king's voice seemed stern.

I decided not to talk to the king and asked my F13A Saber to provide me with some information on how to use it.

After a few minutes of hearing a boring, long and informative audiobook on rope darts, I finally realized how to use it.

I asked the staff to go destroy the massive robot, while I used the rope dart.

I swung it to my left and two robots evaporated into dust. After my killing machine went far enough, I thought, *this rope dart is lighter and it wouldn't harm my wrist as well, and this is easier to handle.*

Then, I almost slashed my eye out.

Okay, this is not at all easy to handle.

We were slashing robots apart easily. Despite having a much smaller army than them, we were winning. I was certain that we had finished more than half of the robots and both the massive ones were destroyed. Roughly, our army and their army had the same number of soldiers.

The good thing was that none of our apes had died. I was successful in protecting them. As we were winning, I wanted to end the battle as soon as possible and get free from all this and go back to my mom... unharmed.

But, as I thought we were winning and there was no chance that they could win, all of a sudden; luck turned the tables on us.

As the red light surrounded them, the metal casing housing the chip shifted into transparent glass, revealing the wires and inner workings of their robotic form. They grew a few centimetres in size. The atmosphere hummed with a strange energy, crackling around their robotic bodies as they underwent this weird transformation.

I had a feeling that our bad times were just about to start.

XXII

THE ULTIMATE FACE-OFF

Till the time I realized what just happened, a laser touched my hand. A clean cut formed on my hand, blood dripping from it.

The blood dripping from my hand reminded me of the dried blood I'd seen on the ground the first day I'd come here.

I felt anger, annoyance and all negative feelings you could ever think of. I was feeling a bit impatient as I thought we were winning but then all of a sudden, we are losing. I swished the rope dart right at the center of its chest and swung it back to me, expecting it to evaporate to dust.

To my surprise, it didn't evaporate into dust. The glass had broken, but the chip was there, exactly where it was supposed to be.

I attacked again and this time my rope dart hit the chip right in the center. This time, I was sure that the robot would evaporate into dust, but the chip itself regenerated.

The robot shot another laser at me, hitting me right below the eye.

I suddenly felt so angry that I totally forgot about destroying the chip. I wanted to take out his hand from its body and kill it with its own hand.

I knew I couldn't kill the robots with the rope dart and so I summoned my killing machine and it protected me from the next laser attack pointed right at my eye.

I took my staff and plunged at the robot's hand, aiming to remove it out of its body. Thanks to the staff's power, I jumped higher and hit the staff right on its shoulder.

Along with the irritation and anger inside me, I used my arm power to remove the arm off the robot. As expected, the arm of the robot fell off from its body and it started to regenerate.

I quickly took the robots hand in my arm and searched for anything that would shoot out the laser. I wasn't positive that this was going to work but I wasn't negative either. If this idea could work, then the battle would be easily won; but if not, I needed to figure out another way.

There was a single red square button on the index finger and I subconsciously pressed it.

Then, a laser shot out of it. I pointed it at the chip, hoping that this would work. As soon as the laser touched the chip, it started to melt and after a few seconds, it completely melted into liquid and the robot disintegrated into dust.

I turned around and just took a step to shout my lungs out and the apes and tell them to do it but then I heard a really annoying sound like a fork screeching a metal bowl.

I turned around and scowled to find the melted metal turned back into a chip and it started to regenerate. Honestly, I was so done with this robot that I wanted to kill it for good; only if I knew how to do it.

When a layer started to form on the chip, I smashed it into pieces with my foot. I was still angry so I pointed the laser at the broken chip and it turned into dust.

It took me moment to realize that when I pointed it the laser at the chip before, it had melted, but now, it turned into dust. *Maybe, I thought, that we needed to destroy the chip twice to finish it once and for all.*

I asked my staff if that if there was any way by which I could send this message to the other apes without having to scream my lungs out. As always, my staff had an idea.

A golden light glowed from the staff and it did its work.

I ran towards a tree where I could hide. Actually, I flew towards it as the snow was quite deep (And by quite deep, I mean very deep).

I went behind the thick trunk of the tree and pointed the robot hand to a robot. My plan was to help the apes while not getting into danger. I knew that that it was really bad and a bit selfish to hide there like a coward when the apes were rising their lives.

I looked around for any ape who needed help. I noticed that almost every ape needed help. Only the king had figured out what to do and was killing the robots with rapid speed.

The king melted one robot's chip and was about to hit it when I did it for him. I don't know how but he always seemed to know that I did it. He looked in my direction and we locked eyes.

I gave a thumbs up to him and thankfully; he understood what to do. The plan was that he would do the first step; melting the chip, and I would do the next part, evaporating it into ashes.

The king kept melting the chips while I waited for a few seconds before the chip reformed.

The king was just about to kill the next robot when I burned a bit of the robot's hand which the king was holding to catch his attention. He turned to look at me and I pointed out that an ape was in danger and I needed to help it.

The king nodded and melted the chip, causing the robot to turn into dust.

I turned to the ape which I'd seen before. I was just about to help when that ape cut of the hand from the robot's body and melted the chip. He crushed it with his foot it evaporated into dust.

Although I was hovering above the snow, the cold was still biting my skin. I almost felt like a spy, keeping a watch on everyone.

I helped kill another robot. Suddenly, I felt stinging pain on my back. I touched my it to find that my white t-shirt was cut. I knew that feeling. I alertly turned around with the robot hand ready to attack.

I found a robot as expected and shot a laser beam at it. It dodged. I pointed it at its chip. Nothing happened, not even a crack.

I realized that this must be some improvised robot. As discreetly as possible, I took my stick and stood up, levitating a few millimetres above the snow. I jumped and hit the staff at the glass where the chip as placed.

I heard metal clank. I tilted my head to find that the robot had stopped the staff from hitting the chip with his hands.

I knew that this was going to be no easy task; so, I started to back away. 'Uhm,' I began, 'I was just fooling around. I had no intention to kill you. I-I am helping you to kill the apes. I-the apes think that I'm on their side, but actually I am on your side. I just killed a-

The robot held me by my neck and lifted me off the ground. I was already off the ground but, okay.

It started to apply more pressure on my neck and I started to choke. My staff and the robot arm dropped from my hands and I was now completely defenceless.

I kicked the robot and it only staggered for a second, loosening his grip a bit. I took the opportunity to escape it. That moment, I freed myself and took the staff before touching the snow. I asked my staff to help me escape from it. I quickly took the robot arm but before I could get away with both of them, the robot got a hold of my boots.

I loved them and didn't want to take them off, but I had no other option. It was a question of boots or life. I chose life. I pulled out my leg from the boot, flying away from the robot. The boot stayed in the robot's hand.

I thought I had escaped the robot when I felt a cool wind blow near my leg, sending a shiver through my body. I looked back to find that the robot was flying, coming towards me with rapid speed.

Faster! I thought. I was starting to get a bit panicked. I didn't know what to do. For a moment, I was completely blank. Then, I got an idea. I left the staff but was still flying with the same speed. I gripped the robot arm tightly in my arms and shot laser at the robot.

He dodged it and shot a laser beam at me, which unfortunately I couldn't dodge. The laser beam hit my right leg, tearing my jeans at the knee. I felt stinging pain in my leg which I was trying not to pay attention to.

The robot shot another laser beam at me which I dodged. It was aimed right at my eye. I sighed and looked at my staff. The laser had got my staff. It was cut in half. Thankfully, the other half that had fallen down came flying towards the half in my hand and mended itself.

I sighed and looked back at the robot. I called out to the staff to give me some strength. After a moment or two, I felt a strange power run through my body and immediately I knew that the staff had done its part.

I was still facing the robot. It shot a laser beam at me and for a second, everything slowed down. The sound of the battle faded from the background, it was only the robot and me.

It shot another laser beam at me and I dodged it with ease. It was almost like he was stuck in slow motion. It was almost as if I was some superhero. Honestly speaking, I felt like Neo from matrix, the only difference was that he was dodging bullets and I was dodging laser beams.

Dodging lasers like that was fun. *Is this speed for a limited time or is it unlimited?* I asked my blunt staff. *It's for a limited time boss. Use it carefully. You only have four minutes before the power extinguishes.* It spoke in my head.

Is there any way that you can extend this power for a-
Three minutes forty-two seconds.
Ugh, fine. But, are you sure that you can't extend the time-
Three minutes thirty-three seconds.

I knew that there was no winning in this battle with the staff no matter how hard I tried. So, I did what I could do.

I wanted this battle to get over as soon as possible. So, I targeted the glass under which the chip was placed and pointed the laser at it. That was still a bit hard as the robot was constantly moving.

After a few seconds of pointing the laser at the robot, it started to crack. The glass was about to break when the robot realized what as happening and started to shoot laser at me. He was shooting at least six or seven laser beams at me at once. Although the laser beams were coming at me in slow-motion, I was still having a bit trouble in dodging all of them.

Instead of flying away from him, I flew closer to him. Before the robot could robot could react to what was happening, I hit my staff in the center off the chest, breaking the glass.

Before I could point the laser beam to the chip, the robot hit me in my left hand with the laser, causing a clean cut on my forearm. I held my left hand and backed away, my insides burning with pain. I had seen that attack coming but it was so sudden that I didn't have the time to react to it.

Boss, two and a half minutes left. It spoke in my head, causing me to put aside my pain and focus on the task in hand.

I flew towards the robot and put my hand inside its chest and took out the chip, evaporating the robot into dust in slow motion. Then, I took the laser-throwing hand and pointed the laser to the chip. That, again, melted in slow motion. Then I realized that I would have to wait for longer time before the chip turned back into itself.

To make this wait a bit shorter, I started to look into the battle, seeing what the other apes were doing. When I looked at them, I realized that there was no sound in the battle and everything was in black and white.

Then, the liquid in my hand started to change into a more solid form and my attention got diverted to it again. Once it had fully converted into a solid form, I crushed it into pieces and everything turned back to normal.

The sound of the chaos, the sound of metal clanging and the apes shouting. Once the sound was there, the colour started to change from black and white. I looked at my hands to see that they were also changing the colour.

I looked at my left arm and the stinging pain returned to my arm. I winced in pain.

I was still staring at my hand subconsciously. Just then, I had a surprised gasp from the apes.

I looked at the battle to see that all the robots were fading on their own. Even the king looked surprised at it.

Well done boss. You killed the head robot. I know that you don't know why these guys are fading. It's because you killed the head robot. The guy that you just killed was the one who was the head of all robots. I think you are smart enough to understand that if you kill the head, you kill all. It spoke in my mind. I felt very proud of myself. A thought then struck me. I was just a normal teenager a few days back. Now, I'm the messiah of guys hundred time my height.

I knew when I would go back to my mum and tell her all this, she wouldn't believe it. If I was in her shoes, I wouldn't either. Actually, I still wasn't sure whether this was reality or was it just a dream.

All the apes looked at me and came hurrying towards me. The all ran to me and I shouted at the top of my lungs, 'It's party time!'

XXIII

I GO FOR A STROLL IN THE MIDDLE OF A JUNGLE

It was still hard to believe that we won the war.

So, as promised, we had two parties back-to-back. One for Edward and one for winning the war. Of course, we didn't do the parties immediately after the battle. We gave the soldiers a few days' time to recover from their injuries.

I was sure that the soldiers were having a good time with their families. But I wasn't having such a great time. Right after the war ended, a few apes carried me to my dressing room and put a vanilla-smelling ointment on my wounds. The worst part is that I had to sleep on my bed for a whole day doing absolutely nothing. I wasn't allowed to walk or run around and no one was allowed in my room. Even my staff was taken away from me and there was absolutely no sign of Coco anywhere.

They took my staff away saying that it would disturb me during my healing process. They said that it was necessary to have complete peace of mind and silence in my surroundings to heal my wounds as soon as possible.

I was okay till the time the vanilla smell was reaching my nose. Then, suddenly, the foul smell of the green ointment started reaching my nose. I wondered where this smell was coming from. I lifted my left arm to see that the vanilla smelling ointment was slowly changing to the smelly green ointment. Honestly, that thing smelled of rotten eggs and meat that was kept out in the sun for a hundred years. I felt pukish.

Normally, I would feel good that there was no one to disturb me, but with this foul-smelling thing that covered my whole body, it was hell. I felt pukish all day and there was no one around.

On that day, I had a lot of time to think about the things that had happened to me in the last few days. I had a lot of time to think about the coming party, about Coco, and about me going home back to my mother. I wondered how they would do that.

I thought I would spend my time by looking out of the window but I got bored after a few minutes. I thought of going back to the room beneath the bathroom but then I didn't have the staff to protect me if I got hurt.

I don't fear the dark but I do fear ghosts like Pennywise, Teke-Teke and Annabelle. It was nightfall. I still couldn't believe that we'd finished such a huge army within half a day. It was unbelievable.

I looked at the clock to see that it was already ten. I looked out to see that it was completely dark now. Nothing was visible at all. It was completely dark and I was in no condition to go and switch off the light.

Suddenly, the lights went off and a shiver went up my spine. Day before yesterday, I was sleeping in the woods and I had been too tired to worry about any ghosts.

Today, I had slept for a while when I drank the hot chocolate and so I didn't need any sleep nor I wanted any. I turned towards the window wall and that sent another shiver up my spine.

My imagination had always been very wild. Whenever I was alone in a new place, I needed someone beside me, even if it was a staff.

The problem was that if I faced towards the window, I felt that pennywise would jump out of nowhere and break the window and eat me. And I used to think that the clown which was always sitting on the bench outside McDonalds was sleeping beside me when I was facing the window. If I turned my back to the window, I used to think the Annabelle or pennywise is watching me.

So, I kept my eyes closed, trying to sleep, trying not to think about those scary ghosts. But, unfortunately, even if I close my eyes, I would see their horrid faces. I decided to sleep with that. But sleep had a long way to come.

I don't know how long I was awake but suddenly, I felt warmth and light on me. I faced towards the window wall to see that dawn was breaking and I still wasn't feeling sleepy and I couldn't stay in the bed for any longer.

I got up and looked at my wounds in the mirror. They had healed completely. Now, the next thing that I had to do was to take a bath and change into fresh and new clothes.

I went inside the bathroom and saw that there was a floral cotton t-shirt and a matching jean which I was quite happy to wear as it was comfortable but it would have been a bit more comfortable if there were shorts or-

Okay, just leave it.

Once I freshened up, I went outside to take a stroll, hoping to meet Coco on the way. I walked for about an hour or so, taking in the fresh smell of the leaves and the mud beneath my feet. I didn't realise how much missed it. Honestly, living in a busy place, you could never possibly find so much greenery and peace of mind. It's always so noisy. There's not a single place in a city where you could have no noise except the calming voice of nature. I wanted my mother to experience this. She would've felt so good, away from the hecticness of her work.

The feeling was so nice when I lost sense of my surroundings and just wanted to live here for the rest of my life. I wanted to go back in time and bring my mum here.

Just then, I heard a rustling of leaves behind me and turned, expecting the staff to be in my hand but then I realized that I didn't have the staff with me.

I agree that I became a bit scared, after all, I was still a school-going teenager who was a nerd.

I clenched my fist, ready to punch any animal in the face. I wouldn't be surprised if a giant sabre-toothed tiger leaped at me from behind the bushes. With that thought, a drop of sweat appeared from my face even though it was quite cold.

From the bushes, Coco came out. He was clenching his stomach and laughing. 'Y-You should've looked at your face.'- he said, still laughing. 'What's so funny about it?'- I asked grumpily.

With that, he laughed even harder. 'Never mind.'- I muttered. 'Anyways, what made you come here?'- he asked, grinning broadly. 'Just came for a stroll.'- I said.

'Oh. Even I came here for a stroll, hoping to meet you.'- he said. I nodded and said, 'You're coming to the party, right?'- I asked.

His expression turned a bit sad and disappointed. 'I don't think that I will be able to come. The party's only for those who fought the war and their families.'- he said. 'Coco, you don't *think* that you'll not be able to come or you don't *want* to come?'- I asked. He didn't reply. 'And anyways,'- I said, 'You can come with me to the party. I can tell that you're my guest. After all, who will stop a messiah?'

Coco smiled and nodded his head.

We started to walk together, back to the palace. While walking, Coco asked me, 'Now that everything is done, how will you go home?' I had not thought of that. I wonder how troubled my mom would be. 'I will talk about that to the king. Thanks for reminding me. I had so much on in my mind that I didn't have time to think about it.'- I lied. I had a lot of time to think about it yesterday. 'I understand.'- he said.

'I'm sure that the king will not take a lot of time to send me back home.'- I said. 'That's right. Two or three days at max.'- he said.

We continued walking when he looked at me carefully as though I was carrying a gun to kill him. 'Where's your F13A Saber?'- he asked. 'I have no idea. Yesterday, they took it away from me while treating my wounds and didn't give it back.'- I said. 'Oh, okay. I think I know where your weapon might be.'- he said. You can always expect these kinds of things from Coco. 'There's no need for that. They will give it to me in the party I guess.'- I said. 'Could be.'- he said.

We didn't talk much for the rest of the way. Once we reached the castle, I asked, 'Hey Coco, where were you when the war was going on?' 'I was hiding somewhere, away from the battle. I surely had a hard time finding my way back. After a day a searching for the palace, I spotted you walking in the middle of the jungle.'- he admitted.

'Cool.'- I said. We stood there awkwardly for a moment and then Coco said, 'Bye.' 'Okay, bye, hope to see you at the party.'- I said, and he went swinging back into the jungle.

Then, a thought struck me. If Coco was a royal prince, then why didn't he stay in the palace with us all? If he was lost in the jungle and was finding his way back to the palace, then why did he go back into the jungle? I thought of asking that afterwards. Right now, I was looking forward to the party.

XXIV
IT'S PARTY TIME!

When I reached my room, fresh clothes for the party were provided to me and they called me down for breakfast.

I never had such a grand breakfast before. It was delicious. The table had a red cloth placed on it and there were king chairs placed beside it. There was a big glass chandelier hanging from the ceiling. There were several dishes placed on the table which were covered.

The table was so big that it could fit almost twenty people, but, only two people were there in the dining room: The king, and Coco.

I sat next to Coco and greeted the king. Coco had changed into a royal attire which looked pretty good on him. The king was in his royal attire. Not the golden one, the brown one. It was the one with the black boots and a woolen jacket.

I noticed that none of them had started eating. When I sat down, three apes came and served us the food. For breakfast, we had sausages, omelets, salad, fruit and fruit juices, toast with butter, French toast, and some traditional food whose name was so complicated that I don't even remember. It was even more complicated than the venom that the robot gave me. But it was surely tastier than the venom.

Once we'd finished our breakfast, the king told us, 'I have sent clothes for the party tonight in your rooms. I believe that you would've got them before breakfast.' We both nodded and he continued, 'The party starts at half past six and most probably go on till eleven or ten. If you wish to leave before, you may go. Dinner starts at sharp seven and ends at eight. Try to come before dinner starts.'- he said and then looked at Coco, 'Be on time, we don't accept latecomers.'- he taunted.

Once we left the dining hall, I invited Coco to my room and we chatted a lot. I think it was an hour or two before he left my room. There was a series of events while I waited for the party. So, I guess that there was nothing interesting or anything that you must know about, so I think we can skip to the part where the party starts.

I started to dress for the party almost thirty or forty-five minutes before it started. I had to wear a white tuxedo to the party.

When I looked at myself in the mirror, for a moment, I didn't think that it was Aiden standing there. I looked so different. I had never worn a tuxedo, until now. I always used to wonder how I would look in a tuxedo. I knew that I had to wear a tuxedo someday, but not today. I was content that I wore it properly.

As always, I was looking amazing. I looked like a gentleman. I saw the time on the clock and noticed that there were only fifteen minutes left for the party. I took one last look at myself in the mirror, straightened my tie, brushed off invisible dust from my suit, and took my combat boots. When I held them in my hands, I realized that this wouldn't go with the outfit.

I looked around for my earphones so that I could ask the king if combat boots were allowed in a formal party. Unfortunately, I couldn't find my earphones, but I found something else.

I found a bow in the place where I used to keep my staff. I kept my combat boots down and opened the box. Much to my surprise, I found new shoes which were perfectly matching with my tuxedo. They were white patent shoes that matched my dress. I wondered what Coco and the king would wear.

I took a look at the time to see that only five minutes were left. I quickly put on my shoes and walked out of the door. Then, I realized that I didn't know where the party was supposed to be.

I walked to the entrance and looked around for any signs of apes in the castle. Luckily, I spotted Coco a few meters away and ran up to him.

Even he was wearing a white tuxedo exactly the same as mine, except that he had a golden batch on the left side of his chest which had a roaring tiger.

We walked to an enormous hall which I had not seen before. It was not hard to imagine that it could fit an army of twenty-thousand apes. (I hope you remember that a single ape is almost thirty times my size, and I'm 5'9.)

Everyone was there except the king. All the soldiers were in black tuxedos. It was quite weird seeing apes in tuxedos and patent shoes. It was kind of weird to see them standing straight and so sophisticated like humans. I asked Coco if the king was present because I couldn't spot him in a crowd of twenty-thousand apes. He told me that the king was not present.

While we were talking, one of the apes spotted me and I waved my hand to them. I spotted Edward in the crowd and walked to him. I hoped that I came to the correct ape because they all looked so similar. 'Congrats once again, Edward. I'm really happy for you.'- I said and shook his hand once again. 'Thank you for helping us win the war. I still can't believe that not a single of our apes died. All thanks to you.'- said Edward. I laughed lightly. 'No, it was not me. It was you guys who did it after all, and the F13A Saber. I was just a helping hand. I mean, just look at the difference between our size.'- I joked. He chuckled and suddenly, all the murmurs died out and all the faces turned to the opposite side. I looked back to see that the king was arriving.

I noticed that even the king was wearing a white tuxedo but he was wearing four or five golden badges, but the biggest was the roaring tiger who was facing sideways. The design of the badge was the same as the one which was etched on his golden armor which he was wearing on the first day I met him.

He spotted me and gestured for me to come out from the crowd. I did as he said- I mean gestured. I was standing to the left of the king and Coco was standing to his right.

When all the faces were turned towards the king, I realized that the king was going to give a speech. I looked at his hand and saw that he was holding a glass with red wine in it.

'My loyal and faithful soldiers,'- he began, his voice loud and clear. 'Today, I stand before you with a heart filled with pride and gratitude. We have emerged victorious in a hard-fought battle. This victory belongs to each one of you who fearlessly stood on the battleground, knowing that you may not survive. This victory belongs to each one of you who stood by our kingdom when we needed you the most. This victory is for everyone who fulfilled their duty in the battleground. But, of course, we didn't do this alone. There's someone special present amongst us today. We have a true hero among us today. He has shown us what true loyalty means.' He put a hand on my shoulder, which was quite heavy. 'I want to thank Aiden from the bottom of my heart. Without him, we would not be celebrating today. Aiden, your courage and sacrifice for us showed us what true loyalty means. Despite being a human, you helped us in the war. You endangered your life for us. I can never fully thank you for what you did. I know that our first meeting was very rough, and I wasn't expecting that you would help us. Our kingdom owes you a debt that we can never fully repay. Let's look forward to a future of peace and happiness, knowing that together, we are strong. United, we are strong. United, we are invincible. United, we are undefeatable. United, we are unstoppable.'- he concluded. 'To our kingdom!' shouted the king enthusiastically, raising his wine glass. 'To our kingdom!'- replied the crowd enthusiastically and raised their glasses.

With that, the king walked down to Edward and patted him on the back. 'And to Edward, our new lieutenant.'- he said loudly. 'To Edward.'- said the soldiers.

The rest of the party, the king personally went and talked to each one of them and their families. There were several groups formed of friends, apes who were seniors from the rest and the young ones; who were still enjoying this time of their lives. I was included in the group where Edward was there. I talked to them for a few minutes and then Coco called me. 'Just a minute.' I said to the group and walked to Coco.

When I got close to him, I noticed that he was holding two glasses, one for me and one for him. (Don't worry, it wasn't wine.) He handed me a glass that was comparatively smaller than his. There was a maroon-colored drink in it. 'What's this?' I asked. 'It's a traditional drink. It is made from a plant. I forgot its name but it's very tasty, try it. It used to be my favorite drink.' He spoke. 'Hang on a minute, what do you mean by *used to be* your favorite drink? What happened now?' I asked. 'Nothing. I drank one more juice recently which I liked a lot, so I'm not able to decide which one is better. Most probably the other one.'- he said thoughtfully. 'Anyways, try it.'- he said enthusiastically. 'It's not beetroot, is it?' I asked. Coco laughed lightly and said, 'No, it's not beetroot. Now try it, will you?' I hesitantly took one sip from the glass and the moment it went down my throat, I felt as though I had drunk the juice for immortality. It was so delicious that for a second I almost felt like I was in heaven. I took one more sip from the glass for a quick reality check. It didn't make me feel any more in reality, but that's okay.

'Coco, you said that you drank a juice that tasted better than this. I want to try it. I can't imagine anything better than this.' I spoke. 'Yes, when I drank this for the first time, even I couldn't imagine anything better than this until I drank that. It was amazing. I can't tell you how good that was. That juice was ten times better and was healthier.' He said dreamily.

I wondered how amazing it would taste. I couldn't dream of anything better. 'Hey Coco,' I said, 'This thing doesn't contain alcohol, does it?' 'No, Dad set this up only for us both.' He spoke.

Before I could say anything else, I heard the king's voice, 'Everyone can now have dinner. The counters are open.' 'Is this a buffet?' I asked Coco. 'What else does it look like?' he asked.

The dinner was even better than the lunch. Oh sorry, I skipped the part where we had lunch. Okay, so the food was smelling so good that it was almost drawing me towards it. Today, I had a heavy breakfast and didn't eat a lot for lunch so I was starving.

Apes queued and took the plates. Me and Coco stood together in the queue. I thought that apes only ate bananas, until now. There was spaghetti, all colors of pasta, pizza, Manchurian, chicken nuggets, burgers, noodles, mac and cheese, chicken and vegetable salad, tofu, fish N' chips, and so many more things that I don't even remember. There was a smaller serving spoon for me.

I wanted to try so many more things but it was just a bit too much for my small tummy. Oh, and I forgot to tell you about the deserts. They were mouth-watering. There were chocolate brownies, ice cream, cheesecakes, chocolate cakes, chocolate cookies, chocolate and vanilla-flavored muffins, chocolate puddings, donuts with a variety of flavors, and tarts.

I and Coco had our dinner while sharing jokes and ideas. All along Coco kept smiling and I couldn't help laughing at the silly faces he kept making. As we were talking, the topics changed from food to dress, dress to craft, craft to war, war to party, and party to the first time we met. 'I never get used to new people so quickly.' Said Coco. 'Same here. When I saw you the first time, I was wondering if it was a trap and if you were trying to kill me because I was still having a hard time believing that I was not dreaming and you guys might kill me.' I spoke. Coco smiled.

'Hey, want to try out the deserts?' I asked. 'Sure.' He replied. We got the desserts and sat down. 'You know,'- I began, my mouth stuffed with the cookies. I swallowed the cookie and spoke again, 'When I entered the court, I saw your father, but I was like, where is the queen? Then, a few days passed, no sign of the queen. Where was she? It had been almost two days when there was no sign of the queen. Did she flee away?' I said jokingly and looked at Coco. The smile vanished from his face. I had hit a nerve.

'Uhm, Coco. I'm sorry, I didn't mean to hurt you. Sorry.' I said, trying to comfort him. 'My mother's gone.' He said bitterly, and I had a feeling that he was going to punch me and I was going to go flying out of the palace.

'I mean, she's not dead, or maybe. My father banished her.' He spoke. 'Is that why your relationship with your father isn't so good?' I asked. 'No. She betrayed him and the kingdom. Some ten years back, father got to know that mother was a spy from the enemy's army. She was here to steal all the ideas, military strategies, and weapons from here. In the middle of the night, Dad caught her sneaking outside the palace and followed her. That's when he found out that she was an enemy. The next day, with a heavy heart, he banished her from the kingdom.' Said Coco.

I couldn't help feeling bad for Coco. 'I'm sorry for whatever happened.' I said softly. 'No,' said Coco. 'She was a traitor. She was never a part of our family. I was only five then and I don't even remember her.' He spoke.

When we were talking about his mom, I remembered something.

'Just give me a minute, Coco.' I said and left to find the king. He was busy talking to Edward and his family. I made my way through the crowd to the king. Till the time I reached him, he was about to move forward to the next family. The king spotted me and stopped. 'Yes Aiden, what is it?' he asked when I was close enough. 'When can I go back home?' I said immediately. I was about to say, *when will you send me home?* But I bit my tongue not to say that as that may sound rude.

The king looked a bit surprised at this sudden approach. 'Two days.' Said the king. 'But you will have to give us your watch as we will need to study it properly in order to send you back to the past.' He spoke majestically.

'No matter how hard I try, I can't take it off.' I said. 'Have you tried the laser beam or try the staff to break it?' he asked. 'No,' I said, 'Not yet, but I will try it. But what if it doesn't come out and I get stuck here forever? What if I'm never able to see my mom again?' I asked nervously. 'Stop overthinking it, Aiden. If it doesn't work, we'll find some other way.' He said confidently.

I left without saying another word, trusting the king to help me go home. However, deep inside me, I still had a question, *If I'm not able to return, what will happen to my mother? Will I grow old without seeing her for the rest of my life? Will I die without seeing her for one last time?* I tried to shove that thought away, but it just wouldn't go away.

XXV

I HEAR A TALE

I made my way through the crowd, still thinking about that not-very-positive-thought and my conversation with the king.

I sat next to Coco and told him that I'd most probably go back in a few days. 'Before you go, I'll make sure that you get to try that drink.' Said Coco. 'Hey, before I go, I want to hear more about your past- I mean, apes' past. You must have some mythological stories, right? I want to hear all of them.' I spoke. 'Sure, I'll tell you one now, if you're okay with that.' Said, Coco. 'Yeah, I'm completely fine with it, but, it's a bit noisy here. Do you want to go outside? It's going to be quieter, so I would be able to listen properly and understand it better.' I spoke.

'It's one of my favorites. I guess you'll like it. I feel that it's one of the most interesting stories I've ever heard.' Said Coco.

Me and Coco went outside and he set a fire to keep us warm as it was still a bit cold. We sat facing each other. There was a log on which we sat. I had a bit of trouble sitting on it as it was quite high.

'So,' I said, 'What's the story about?' and moved a bit closer to the fire. 'It's a story about a messiah. Usually- almost every time apes are the messiahs, but there are only two human messiahs in ape history. One is you, and the other is who this story is about.' He spoke. 'I don't know if this story is real or if it's just a kid's—'

'Just tell me.' I said impatiently.

Coco paused and stared at me for a while which gave me the chills because of the fire and the darkness around it. 'Can, you stop giving me that look?' I said, sounding like a total scaredy cat. 'I don't know, can I?' he said, still giving me that creepy stare.

I moved a bit away from Coco. Seeing my discomfort, he said, 'Okay, so the story is set somewhere between 2160 and 2200.' He paused and looked at me to make sure that I was listening. 'After the humans first made the robot, as I've told you before, they made an army to kill the apes. There was a malfunction, no scientist pressed the wrong button or something like that. So, the malfunction caused the robots to kill the apes as well as the humans. Most of them died in the war because of the destruction, and the robots killed the rest.' He spoke.

But before he could continue, I interrupted him and said, 'Hey, the chip that made the apes think and act like humans, that was only there in those who were experimented by us. Then how are you guys able to communicate like us? You guys don't have any chips inside you, right?'

Coco thought for a while and said, 'Uhm, no, we don't have chips inside us.' 'Then how are *you* able to communicate and act like humans?' I asked. 'Hmm,' he said, 'Nice question. The answer to that is...' he paused and thought for a few seconds.

'Okay, yeah, got it. Now, how should I explain it to you?' he paused again and said, 'So when the chip was put inside the apes who were experimented, their body underwent a change. Their DNA changed along with several other things. The apes who were experimented on died of old age and the others examined one of the ape's DNA and replicated it. They saved it for future generations so that they won't have to undergo painful surgery to behave and talk like humans.' Said Coco.

'But why did you need intelligence like humans?' I asked inquisitively. 'We needed intelligence similar to the humans to defeat the robots. If we were normal apes, we could've never had such technology and weapons, which were needed to defeat the robots, and we did it.' He spoke. 'With your help, of course.' He added hesitantly.

I blinked at him and kept staring for absolutely no reason. With that, he said, 'Do you want to listen to the story I was going to tell you, or do you want me to save it for tomorrow?' breaking the staring competition between us.

I thought for a while and said, 'I guess I can't wait till tomorrow evening, nor do I have the patience. So, I will hear it now.'

'Fine then. I'll tell it to you now.' Said Coco. 'Okay, so the malfunction caused the robots to destroy the humans. The battle between us raged on for one year, ten months, and twelve days.' He spoke. 'Oh my God, it was almost two years.' I couldn't help myself interrupting the story.

'The battle raged for months and we were losing badly. The apes only had a handful of apes. They were only left in hundreds, most of them were women and children. They decided that safety was first, and went into hiding. They only attacked if necessary. Then, a normal day was going on in their lives. Well, I would not call it a normal day, but anyway. A human appeared from nowhere, with two apes. We knew that he could do us no harm, unless, he brought an army of robots with him. he was certainly very small, but anything could be a threat, so they decided to kill him. But before they could kill him, he said that he wanted a last wish before he died. They granted him the wish and he said that he wanted to show something to them. They heard the rustling of leaves. They kept their spears handy, just in case they got attacked. But, much to their surprise, he had brought an army of apes. They were in thousands. They came out of hiding and challenged the robots. With the advanced weapons and war strategies of the human and the apes, they finally won the war, but those guys kept coming back. I hope that they don't come again this time. Yeah, and that human was wearing a golden watch similar to yours. So, they called him their messiah, our savior. After they won the war, neither the army nor the boy were ever seen again. The apes left them the advanced weapons. The boy was around sixteen or seventeen. We never got a chance to give him a proper goodbye and a thank you. Our search for that guy is still going on. We did find a "missing poster" with the guy's photo and name on it. The name was not that clear, although. It was almost as if both the army and the boy had come from the future to save them. But that couldn't have been possible as we are still working on a time machine which is probably going to be done in the next few months, or maybe years.' He finished.

I was still wondering who that guy must be. He must have been so brave to go between apes who were ready to kill him.

While I was wondering all that, Coco asked, 'Do you want to hear more stories, or is this enough for today?' 'I guess this is okay. Anyways you'll be taking me to taste that juice you were talking about.' I spoke. 'If Father does not have any other tasks in hand for us.' He added.

'So, what should we do now?' I asked him. He thought for a while and said, 'Do you want to have another round of dessert?'

'Sure, why not?'

XXVI
I DRINK THE HEAVENLY JUICE

After we had the dessert, I went to sleep with my stomach hurting because of overeating. That was the first night I had a good night's sleep and woke up fresh.

I went into the bathroom to brush my teeth. I took a bath and changed. I opened the bathroom door to see Coco reading a book on my bed.

'Hey Coco, I didn't know you would be here so soon.' I spoke. 'Me neither.' He muttered, still reading the book. 'So, are we ready to go?' I asked.

He closed the book and we went out. I was expecting to go swinging or by a horse-driven carriage. But, to my surprise, we went in a car. A royal car made specially for the royal blood.

I was sleeping for almost half the drive. Coco had told me that that place was almost two hours away from the kingdom. I thought that it was stupid just to go so far just to drink some juice.

However, when we reached there, all my anxiety and negative thoughts that were worrying me vanished. It was a beautiful place. It was greener than any place I'd seen around the kingdom. The flowers were not humongous, so I could pluck them and smell them.

They smelled amazing.

The ape who was to give us the drink briefed us about the drink. The drink was made up of flowers and medicinal herbs. All I remember is that one of the flowers was roses and the others had some complicated names.

The drink was refreshing. It was surely way tastier than the beetroot juice. When I heard *medicinal herbs*, I couldn't help thinking that the drink would not be as good as I'd expected. There were also some disgusting ingredients in it (which I will not tell you, or there are chances that you might want to puke). Surely, I was proven wrong.

With every sip, I thought I was in heaven, and when it went into my stomach, I was dragged back to reality. I felt as though I died, went to heaven, had a cup of tea with Jesus, and came back to earth.

It was that good.

***

When we were back in the palace, the taste of drinking heaven was still tingling in my mouth.

Once I'd changed into more comfortable clothes, Coco was inside my room with my staff in his hand.

Hello, old buddy. I missed you. I thought.

Missed you too, boss. Spoke a voice in my head. I couldn't help smiling at this familiar sound in my mind.

'You guys can talk to each other. I'll leave.' Said Coco. 'No,' I said immediately. 'There's no need to go, you can stay here.' I spoke. He smiled and said, 'I just came here to give you your weapon. I was just about to leave when you came out of the bathroom.'

Then, he left my room.

'Where were you, my friend? All these days. You must have felt bored.' I spoke as I sat next to my staff placed on my bed.

After a few moments, it spoke in my head, *I was locked up in a room so dark that even my bright golden light couldn't be seen in it. I was tied up with chains that I couldn't melt. Today, when I had completely given up and was ready to live my life in this dark room, away from everyone, Coco came in, drinking something. He opened me up and we together came here. Happy ending!*

I chuckled at the way he said that. He said it in a way that made me think that he was getting tortured.

'Maybe, my friend,' I said. 'This may be happy, but I'm sure that this is not the end.'

XXVII

WE WASTE A LOT OF TIME

After I had gotten my stick back, I started to try different ways of taking out the watch. Although I was in quite a hurry to go home, I was too lazy to take out the watch by myself.

First, I tried to break the watch with the staff. No luck. Then, I tried to use the hammer to break the watch. (Don't ask me where I had gotten the hammer from.) It didn't come out.

For a moment, I had a feeling that there was no way in which we could remove the watch from my hand. What if the watch had stitched itself to my skin, and to take the watch out, we had to cut the skin underneath it?

That thought horrified me, so I decided not to think about that. After a few moments of thinking, I realized that there was only one option left now. I then started to think of more ideas just in case that didn't work.

I took the robot hand which I had kept in the underground room. Fortunately, that worked and the watch came out.

I took the watch and gave it to the king in the evening. I wanted to go home as soon as possible. I was missing my mom, imagining her condition when she found out that her beloved son had vanished from his bed.

The king examined the watch and said, 'Two days, or maybe more.' With that, he moved towards the 'secret' lab. I wanted to follow him but then I decided not to.

While the scientists were examining the watch, me and Coco spent a lot of time together. I was also able to make their father-son relationship better.

One morning, I woke up to the sounds of loud knocking on the door. I was still in my night suit. I took a few minutes to brush my teeth and not look sleep-deprived.

I opened the door to find Coco standing outside. 'What are you doing here at this time? It's only seven-thirty.' I spoke sleepily. 'I've got good news. Dad told me that once you go, I will become the king.' He said proudly.

'Then I'd rather not go.' I muttered. 'Is that it, or have you got something else to say?' I asked him. 'No, that's pretty much it.' He spoke.

I was so sleepy that I slammed the door shut on his face, which I later regretted. He didn't talk to me for the whole day. I couldn't find him anywhere. When I finally found him after an hour or two of searching, I saw him eating strawberries and talking to some other apes.

I apologized to him and then, I took him out for dinner to his favorite place in the kingdom. (Which I had got to know by asking several servants, soldiers, and the king)

Then, me and Coco had a lot of time to waste when the king told us that it was going to take longer than he thought it was going to take. One part of me was still wondering if I had to stay here forever, and the other was telling me to spend as much time as possible with Coco.

We did a lot of time pass, so we can fast forward that part. Now, if you're thinking that this is the end, you are wrong. I know that people get bored if the happy ending is a bit too long. Something is coming up. No more spoilers, I guess that this is enough to keep you engaged till the end.

The next five days passed in a blur. I don't even recall what happened in those days. So, I guess we can do a little time skip before I start with the next bit of the story.

FIVE DAYS LATER

XXVIII
THE SECRET LAB

I was just chilling in my bedroom when I heard a knock on my door. I walked lazily and opened the door. I saw two apes standing very calmly and in a sophisticated manner on my door. They looked at me and said, 'His Highness is calling you and he says that the wristwatch is ready.'

The moment I heard that, I felt overwhelmed with joy. I wore my combat boots and took my stick with me. I kept following them until we reached the other corner of the palace. We stopped in front of a wall, and for a moment I thought that we were going to run toward the wall and we would go right through it like Harry Potter. I wouldn't be surprised if the wall turned into cotton and we floated over it to the other side of the wall. It was not hard to imagine such things happening here.

While I was imagining stuff, one of the apes put his hand on a very random place on the wall. We waited for a while but nothing happened.

Then, a keypad appeared from the wall and the ape typed a ten-digit code on it. There was a beep sound and then I heard some mechanical whirring.

After that, a handle appeared from the wall and the both the apes pulled it together and pulled the handle. The wall was a door. The moment it opened; a cool breeze engulfed us all which made me shiver.

The stick in my hand glowed red, for the first time and I suddenly felt it growing warmer in my hand. Then, I suddenly felt warmer. I then realized that the staff was keeping me warm. I looked inside to find a dimly lit corridor with a few flickering tube lights. I suddenly had the feeling that they were taking me to the secret lab, where they were going to experiment on me, and going to torture me to death. Then, I remembered that apes were not supposed to be this calm, when they got angry, they could kill you.

I decided to keep that thought aside for now. I then had another thought, when I looked closely, the corridor looked like an underground bunker for zombie apocalypse. Honestly speaking, that unending tunnel looked quite creepy and eerie even at three in the afternoon.

The apes walked into the unending tunnel and I stepped after them. They closed the door with all their might, and then suddenly, the dimly lit corridor turned so bright that I had to cover my eyes before they could burn. The lights were blinding.

One of the apes gave me glasses to wear and said, 'Wear these, if you open your eyes without wearing these, your eyes will burn and you won't be able to blink them. First, your eyes will start to water, and then they would bleed.' That was more than enough for me to know how important it was to wear these special set of glasses.

Once I'd worn them, I opened my eyes and looked around. The dimly lit corridor had now vanished, and in its place was a big room, with flashing (and blinding) white lights. I saw the king, and Coco, who I wasn't expecting to be here. He and the king smiled at me and I walked to them.

I looked around and took a good look at the lab. As expected, it was filled with chemicals of different varieties, there were test tubes, droppers, computers, animals like guinea pigs, hamsters, rats, ants, earthworms, roaches and many other creatures which I was seeing for the first time. They didn't look like they were from earth. Maybe, there was a possibility that they had discovered life in outer space, maybe they had met aliens.

The king handed me the watch and asked me to wear it. Once I'd worn it, I realized how much I was going to miss all the fun with Coco and the time I spent with the king. I took a deep breath and looked at the watch. The king noticed my nervousness and told me, 'Me and Colson will be coming with you to escort you home safely.' I looked and Coco and he nodded.

'You turn the time on the watch to 7:50 when I tell you to,' said the king commandingly. I nodded and the king put his hand on mine, then Coco put his hand on the king's. 'Now.' said the king and I turned the time to exactly 7:50.

XXIX

WE ALMOST TRAVEL AT THE SPEED OF LIGHT

The next thing I know is that we're all flying. It's like that feeling when you jumped from a plane with a parachute. Every part of my body which the wind was hitting, it felt as though someone was pricking needles in my body.

After a few seconds, I felt my body heat up more than it usually should have; and in that second, I had the feeling that I was going to light up like a meteoroid falling from space.

Just when I thought I was going to become a fireball, I stopped flying but kept levitating in air. Then, Coco and the king landed on their feet softly, but I came crashing down right on my face.

I heard Coco laugh, but the king came to my aid.

When the king helped me to my feet, I realized how much worse the injury would have been if we fell down at the same speed from which we flying. Wait, we weren't flying, we were actually falling.

'Just so that you know,' said Coco, 'we were falling at almost the speed of light.'

I laughed.

'What's so funny?' he asked. 'It's impossible for any person to travel at *almost* the speed of light, and not die.' I spoke. 'With our technology, we can.' Said the king. 'Stop exaggerating it. Travelling at only one percent the speed of light can take a lot of energy.' I spoke. Coco spoke, 'I never said that we travelled at the speed of light, I said that we almost travelled at the speed of light. I guess that's some, uh... twenty to twenty five percent. That is around –'

'Twenty-one billion, five hundred eighty-five million, fifty-six thousand, nine hundred seventy-six.' Said the king majestically.

My mouth popped open. I didn't know how long my mouth was open, but I closed my mouth when I realized that saliva was going to come out if I didn't close it. 'Woah,' I said, impressed, 'that's quite a big number.' The king smiled. 'How did you do this, I mean,' I was lost for words, 'it's incredible.'

'I'm afraid I can't tell you how we did this as this is a secret that I can't share with you.' Said the king. 'It's fine.' I said disappointed. But still, I was fascinated by this whole 'travelling at the speed of light' thing.

'Anyways,' I said, 'have we reached?'

'Yes.'

XXX

I WANT MOMMY

I was very excited to see Mum. I took a good look around to see if I remembered the place. I looked around for a few minutes before realizing where I was. 'We are in the garden near my home.' I muttered to myself. I looked up and noticed that it was early morning, around six or seven.

I exited the garden and looked around.

Nothing was the same. I could see my room's window right in front of me. I could see it just a few meters away. I was imagining it. My house was not there, nor were any other buildings. All I could see was a deserted area with scattered trees. There was blood all over. The buildings which I could see were either destroyed completely or were on fire. There were no screaming noises, just the cold wind which sent a shiver up my spine.

I stared into nothingness, looked around for any signs of civilization, looked around for any living creature, looked around for... Mother.

I was in tears. I felt lost and alone. I didn't know what to do. I was scared. I felt like a baby crying for his mommy. I was afraid, I was clueless, and I didn't know where I was. I then felt a tear fall down my cheek onto the ground.

I didn't want mom to die. She was my life; I couldn't live without her. I had no purpose to live if she was not there. I took a few shaky breaths and consoled myself. However, deep down, I wanted to cry. I thought I felt this way since I couldn't spot my mom after coming such a long way just to see her. I felt disappointed. I wanted to punch the king right in the face, but after thinking logically, I realized that my arm was the size of his pinkie finger, and I couldn't even reach his chest after jumping my highest, so... yeah.

I pulled back my tears and went to the king. He was smiling, and for a desperate moment, I thought that he was a robot disguised as a king. I took a few steps back just in case if the king attacked, and if he did so, I would have a few seconds to react (yeah, I'm not that dumb main character who you usually see in movies, who has no brains and even a pre-schooler would know what to do in situations like those).

'What's wrong Aiden, is everything all right?' asked the king after looking at my expression. I must have turned red after crying.

When I didn't reply for a while and looked at the ground, the king seemed to realize what must've happened. He looked out from the entrance and looked around. He didn't say anything but seemed to know exactly what had happened. I thought I knew what was happening but didn't want to agree to it.

'Is there a chance,' I began quietly, and the king turned towards me, 'that we have arrived a bit later in time than we were supposed to be arriving?' I asked. The king looked down and said, 'I'm afraid what you are saying is true.'

Coco kept silent.

At this point, my eyes were filled with water and I couldn't see what was in front of me. 'Is there a chance that,' I began once again, my voice breaking, 'I might never see my mom ever again?' I felt stupid after saying that. I was holding back my tears; they were about to fall on my cheeks.

'No, it's not that.' Said Coco suddenly. 'I guess we came exactly where we were supposed to be but the wrong time. Don't get discouraged, we can always go back and ask them the correct time.' He spoke. I wiped my tears and looked at the king hopefully. He nodded and we gathered around.

The king asked me to change the time on the watch and I did so. I closed my eyes and waited for the falling sensation to come, but it didn't. I opened my eyes to find that both the king and Coco were confused as well.

'What happened?' I asked, my eyes half swollen because of crying. My eyes were half open. 'I don't know.' Said the king. He took out the watch from my hand and tapped it a few times and tried to change the time on the watch, but no luck. I felt the tears starting to rush back to my eyes. I forced them back and tried to act brave and tough, 'Now what?' I kept my voice from cracking up.

'I guess we have no other choice but to stay here and find a way to fix this thing.' Muttered the king. 'WHAT? YOU MEAN THAT WE STAY IN THIS JUNKYARD AND LIVE THE REST OF OUR LIVES HERE?' I wanted to say, but I bit my tongue. I wanted to say a lot more, which you certainly don't want to know. (You would be shocked if I told you. I had a lot of curses in my mind at that point.)

'We just need to find the right tools which are needed to fix this watch.' Said Coco with a slight smile, but I knew that behind that smile, he was scared, he was afraid, the same way I was. 'What will we find in this junkyard?' I said, trying not to sound too rude. 'We will find something or the else here,' said the king. 'Hopefully.' He added silently.

I pretended not to hear that. 'Okay,' I spoke, 'What should we do now?' Both of them kept silent for a while. Then, Coco spoke, 'First of all, we need to know which time we have arrived in. I know that this is not the future, and I must know something or the else about it.' He looked at me and the king. 'But, how do we find that out?' I asked. King and Coco exchanged a look that I didn't understand.

The king closed his eyes and kept them like that for some time. I didn't speak as I knew that this was something important that I didn't need to poke my nose into.

After a few minutes of silence, the king spoke, 'We are in the year 2168.' and opened his eyes. Coco seemed to know exactly what to do. He suddenly looked at me and said, 'Do you remember the story I told you after the party?'

'What party?' I asked stupidly. After a few seconds, I realized that he was talking about the party we had after we won the war. Coco gave me a disappointed look. 'Yeah, what about it?' I asked. 'I told you that it was set somewhere between 2160 and 2200, right?' he said. 'So?' I asked, urging him to continue. 'So,' he said, 'that there is a chance that the messiah will come to save us all and we can ask him to help us get back in time. As this watch is not working, we can ask him to help us get back with his watch.' He concluded.

I looked at him and kept staring at him for a few seconds. I just stood there without any motion and stared at Coco. A lot was going on in my mind so it took me a few seconds to understand what he had said.

'So,' I began irritated, then, I realized that I would start shouting in some time if I didn't control myself. I left out a humorless chuckle and continued, 'You mean that we stay here and wait here for maybe fifty years or more for that stupid messiah to come and save us all, huh?'

The king looked at me and said, 'Aiden, we all are worried and scared, calm down or I will lose my temper. Trust me, you don't want to know how rude I can become when I'm angry. I hope you know how dangerous an ape can be when he's angry.' He smiled, but it was not comforting at all, it was a warning smile, asking me to control myself.

Coco exchanged a look with me that suggested that I should apologize, or I would be thrown with such a speed that I would be able to time travel again.

I got his message and looked down at my feet, and muttered 'sorry'. (it's really hard to say sorry when you mean it. My lips weren't moving, but I forced them to say it.)

The king smiled and said, 'Then, what are we waiting for? Let's go and find the other apes. Maybe they can help us to fix this watch.'

XXXI

I GET INFECTED BY POISON

All of us carefully stepped out of the park and looked around before going ahead. When we saw that the coast was clear, we moved ahead.

My mood became a bit better when I heard that we were going to find other apes. I kept looking around for any signs of robots. The coast was clear.

I don't know how long we walked, but it felt as though we had walked for hours. We'd arrived here at around five or six in the morning, and now, the afternoon sun was right above my head. I was sweating like crazy. I couldn't help asking Coco, 'I'm very tired. When are we going to reach wherever we're going?' I know I sounded a bit annoyed. But I will agree that the king and Coco had excellent patience for they were not crying and getting annoyed by the heat of the sun like me.

'It's only a few minutes travel from here.' Said Coco. 'How many minutes?' I asked. But I was still a bit happy that he didn't say hours.

'It's only three hundred minutes from here.' Said the king, and grinned at me. 'What?!' I almost shouted, exasperated. 'Just joking.' He spoke. 'Phew.' I sighed. 'Its not three hundred minutes from here, it only five hours away.' Said Coco. 'But that's the same thing!' I exclaimed. 'Yes.' Agreed Coco.

After a few hours of travelling, (five hours and thirty-two minutes to be precise) we reached a forest. It didn't look like a very thick one, so we went in without caution, which was a mistake.

The moment we stepped in, my leg got stuck in something and before I knew, I was hanging upside-down. I tried to untie the knot when I realized that there were several spike-like branches surrounding me, and if I moved even a bit, the spikes would poke me and it would bleed to death.

Just to check how sharp it actually was, I put my index finger on the spike. I just touched it, and I could see a few drops of blood on my finger. But the thing that really surprised me was that this was paining like crazy. I noticed that something green was starting to appear around it.

I didn't know what that was, but I surely knew that that was not good. I took a glance at all of the pointy branches around me and noticed that all of the branches had a green coloured pigment on all of them. For a moment, I thought that it was chlorophyll, but then I felt stupid for thinking that as why would anyone put chlorophyll on spiky branches that were meant to kill a person?

Then, I realized what could this be.

It was poison.

However, I was not quite sure whether the poison would kill me right away, or would make me feel immense pain at first and then I would die. I didn't want to die so soon; I wasn't even a complete adult.

Fortunately, the king and Coco had realised that I was not there and were calling out my name. 'I'm up here.' I shouted as loud as I could, my voice now cracking up because of the stinging pain in my finger. I wasn't even sure if any of them heard me.

I took a look at my finger to see arzat my whole finger was already covered in the green pigment. It was as if it was infecting my blood, running through my blood vessels. I knew that this was not good, and I also knew that I needed to stop this before it reached my heart.

I called out to the king and Coco once more and thankfully, they heard me. Coco looked up and pointed towards me. The king looked at me and smiled, I didn't know why, it didn't seem funny.

The king took out a pocket knife, (I wondered if he carried it everywhere) and threw it towards me, but before it could reach me, it bounced back of something. Some force field.

The king then looked at the stick beside his leg. He took my staff and threw it up, and my weapon flew right through the force field and cut the rope on my leg. I fell flat on my stomach, with rocks all around me. Luckily, none of them were sharp enough to stab me, so I was okay.

'Are you okay?' asked Coco, concerned.

'Does he look okay?' asked the king.

I showed them my hand and they both gasped. 'Oh no.' muttered Coco.

The king, on the other hand, didn't waste any time and started to untie the rope on my leg. Once he was done with that, he tied the rope tightly on my hand so that the poison won't spread.

They both helped me get up and we walked together, with the king carrying me. We kept looking out for traps. While the king was holding me, I suddenly felt dizzy and faint. I was very tired so I decided to sleep, or faint. Or maybe it was a heatstroke. God knows what it was.

XXXII
FIRE IN MY BLOOD

I don't know for how long I had passed out, but when I did, it was dark, it was pitch black. I wasn't able to see anything. When I looked around, I saw my stick glowing beside me. I tried to see in the dark, but I couldn't spot Coco or his father.

'Where are they?' I ended up asking my staff. *They've gone to get some food.* Spoke a voice in my head. I sat up straight with a bit of difficulty.

My whole body was in pain. I still felt sleepy and faint. I woke myself out of sleep and exhaustion. It felt as though someone was slowly taking all my energy out of my body. Maybe it was because of the poison.

I took a look at my hand to see that the venom had been blocked by the tight rope that the king had tied around my wrist.

My whole palm felt numb. Maybe because of zero blood flow or because of the poison. My whole palm had turned green, and it looked quite scary. It didn't look as if someone had painted your hand green. When I looked at the back of my hand, I noticed that my veins were popping out from my hand.

I just touched one of my veins which was popping out of my hands. It was surely a very foolish thing to do.

The place where I had touched my vein, it began to turn red. Blood red. It began to change into the colour of my blood.

Then, very slowly, the red colour started to come out of my skin. At first, it only made a whole barely the size of the point of the needle. Then, it started to turn into a bigger hole. Blood shot out of my vein like a poison, right on my face, just below my eye. I very well knew that if a vein was cut, and firm pressure was not applied on it, it would lead to blood loss, and then death. The person would turn pale.

I winced in pain. I wanted to shout, but no sound came out of my mouth. I bit my lower lip to stop myself from screaming in pain and gripped my poison-infected palm with my other hand.

Now that was another mistake I did. I held on to my poisoned hand until the pain had reduced, and I was aware that the bleeding had reduced as well. It didn't die out, but it had reduced.

I removed my hand from the poisoned palm to take a look at it. Blood was still slightly oozing out, but it was paining quite a lot.

Then, suddenly, my whole palm started to turn red. Blood red. It was turning into the colour of my blood. The outline of my fingers was visible on my poisoned hand. I experienced the same pain again, except that it was even more painful. I made sure not to touch my palm this time. I bit my lower lip even harder. I put my other hand on the ground and gripped the magical stick as hard as possible. I shut my eyes close. The feeling was agonizing.

It felt as though someone set fire to my blood.

I opened my eyes and saw that blood was still coming out of my hand at the same speed. I felt myself growing weaker and weaker by the second. I knew I couldn't hold my hand so I placed it on the ground and dug my nails into it. Another mistake of mine.

Before my blood stained the ground, I noticed that the rope on my hand was stained with my blood as well, and the poison.

The blood was travelling from the rope to my hand, and so was the poison. Although I was panicked, I knew what to do. I started to untie the tight knots that the king had done.

The poison was starting to spread rapidly around the rope. I tried to undo the knots as fast as possible, but they were way too tight. I took my stick and ordered it to burn it. Golden light glowed from the wooden stick and I put it on the rope.

That rope fell down on the ground right before the poison could reach my forearm. The poison was now gone from my hand but it was still bleeding.

I looked at both my hands, one of them was bleeding and on the other hand, there were impressions of the staff's etched markings on my hand, indicating how tightly I had held my magical weapon.

Run. spoke a voice in my head.

'What?' I asked out loud.

RUN! said the magical stick in my head, and this time it was loud and clear enough for me to hear and obey it without the need of any explanation, or any reason.

I turned around and started to run, as fast as I could.

Why are we running?

Stop thinking, and run faster. I'll tell you afterwards.

Fine. Wait, how can I stop thinking, man?

I kept running until the time I couldn't run any more. I slowed down. I panted; a drop of sweat appeared on my face. I kept persuading the staff to tell me why we were running. 'And anyways, you're weighing me down.' I told it, still jogging. 'You can fly.' I spoke.

I left the staff and was not surprised to find it levitating in mid-air beside me. 'Can you at least tell me what we're running from?' I asked.

No.

I rolled my eyes in annoyance.

I kept looking back to see what we were running from, but I couldn't see anything. The last bit of energy was draining from me. Finally, the staff glowed a golden light from it, and I understood why. I looked back to see that the poison had spread, and it was coming towards me. I saw it infect a tree, and the moment it touched the tree, all the leaves shed form the tree and the tree collapsed, turning into dust before it even touched the ground. So, we were running from the poison. All of this was happening just because I touched a needle-like branch because I was curious.

Amazing.

I kept running until I bumped into something. My whole face was now covered in sweat. I looked up to find Coco. I was never happier to find him. He looked at me and his attention was fixed upon my sweaty face, he said, 'What happened Aiden? What are you running from? What's chasing you? Is it some giant animal? Why do you look so tired and pale? Can I help? Are you okay? Do want to eat something? Shall I—'

'No time to explain, so just shut up and run!' I exclaimed. I didn't need to say it again.

While running, we spotted the king the king not far away. Looking at us run, he didn't ask any questions, which I was glad for, and ran with us.

We kept running for a few more minutes, and my legs had started to fail me. They were starting to pain. I even twisted my ankle while running, and that was not helping me to run faster. I was left behind by both of them.

Looking at them, and their size, I felt that they were hardly running, they were literally just jogging. There one stap would land almost two hundred meters away. I, on the other hand, was running at my fastest and was managing to stay away from the poison by an inch.

I looked at my staff which was levitating beside me. I mentally slapped myself for not thinking of this before. Of course, as I had no personal space, the stick knew what I was thinking and came closer to me. I held the staff with my right hand, which was not poisoned, and it lifted me into the air.

The king and Coco saw this and did the same. For the first time, the stick grew to almost two meters long to provide sufficient space for all of us to hang on it. I don't know how that was possible because I was told that this thing could only grow five feet, and not more than that.

The king was on my right and Coco was on my left. We were all hanging on the staff with only our hands. I must agree that the king and Coco had a lot of arm strength, maybe because they were apes.

You guys are quite heavy, you know that, right? Spoke a voice in my head. I smiled slightly and looked at the starry sky above me. The moon seemed to look a bit bigger from here. *How high are we in the air?* I asked the stick in my head. *We are thirty-two kilometres above the ground.* Spoke the stick in my head.

Ooh, that's quite high. I thought.

'Guys,' I said, and they all looked at me, 'Hold on tight, and maintain your grip, because a fall from here would be lethal.'

XXXIII
THE KING BREAKS UP A FIGHT

After a minute after we entered the air, my hand started to pain because the carvings of the wooden stick were digging into my skin. 'Can we stop somewhere nearby? My hand hurting.' I said out loud.

The staff took a sharp turn which almost caused me to loosen my grip on it. Once we were stable again, I tightened my grip on the staff. Just after a few seconds, we stopped to reach a mountain cliff and decided to stop there for the night.

Once we'd reached there, I relaxed my arm which was holding me up in the air, and inspected the arm which was bleeding because of the poison.

'I won't die because of blood loss, right?' I asked the wooden stick. It did not say anything but it scanned my bleeding palm. After a few seconds, the voice spoke in my mind, *if it continues to bleed like this for three days, then, you might die. Actually, you will die. I can guarantee you that, a hundred and one percent.*

I didn't say anything for a while. 'When I first heard you, you weren't this rude, or so sarcastic.' I spoke.

Trust me, I'm never gonna call you 'boss' ever again. Itspoke in my head.

I'm not asking you to.

Even if I do, that means I still respect you, and that's never going to happen. I mean, calling a kiddo like you 'boss'? Disgusting.

I groan.

He didn't reply. 'Anyways, can you tell me what these etched markings mean?' I asked.

No. spoke a voice in my head. (See? This is what I'm talking about.) *It's too complicated for you to understand.* It spoke in my head. 'Okay,' I say, 'if you can't tell me what it says, can you at least tell me what language it is in?' trying not to lose my cool.

It's the language we use. It spoke in my head. 'But right now, we're speaking in English.' I spoke.

'Hey,' we were interrupted by Coco. 'What?' I asked in an annoyed tone. 'I've got some herbs which will help heal your wound and reduce the bleeding.' He spoke. 'Oh, yeah, okay, sure.' I say, and lift my hand for him to get a look at. 'Ooh, that's quite deep. It might take a bit of time to heal.' Said Coco, concerned. 'I'm not sure if this will heal it completely, it might leave a scar for a lifetime.' He spoke. I allowed him to apply it to my wound. It pained every time Coco touched it. After he was done, we wrapped it with some leaves that we could find there.

I looked for a comfortable place to sleep and lied down there. Although my Saber was quite rude to me, it still provided me with warmth. I fell asleep almost immediately.

I wondered whether the poison would come here or if would it infect the whole earth. I had nightmares about it... Nightmares that my mother had gotten killed because of that.

I woke up to the sound of Coco and the king calling my name. 'You drool when you sleep.' Said Coco. *You look like the sleeping beauty who is very ugly.* Said a voice in my mind. *That's surely a very beautiful thing to say to a person the moment they wake up. So, thank you. Good morning to you too.* I thought bitterly.

'Good morning, Aiden.' Said the king. I was happy that at least the king knew what to say to a person the moment they woke up. 'I hope you had a good night's sleep.' He spoke.

'Good morning. Yes, I did have a pretty good sleep yesterday. I didn't even need a pillow or a bed to fall asleep. After all that running, I was very tired, and fighting the poison had also taken up a lot of strength.' I spoke.

'That's fine, and how's your wound now?' asked Coco. 'It's better.' I said, looking at it. 'It's not paining much, but I prefer not using the hand too much today.' I spoke.

'Anyways, what are the plans for today?' I ask. 'Today,' said Coco, 'We'll find the apes who are fighting. If I'm correct, they will be in hiding, to protect themselves from the robots. We will also need to be cautious as the robots will be out searching for us, and if they find you, a human, they will instantly kill you. They will kill us as well.' He spoke. 'Agreed.' I say, 'We should probably move.'

We walk through the deep forest, making sure that there's no sign of poison anywhere. I wondered why the poison didn't spread and infect the whole earth, but then, I was broken out of my dream world and pulled back into reality, as Coco pulled me behind a tree.

'What's wrong?' I ask. 'Robots.' Whispered Coco. We keep as still as possible.

After a while, they went and the king said, 'They must've got to know that the apes are somewhere near, so we are quite close now.'

As we continued to walk, I said, 'Why do we even need to find them?' 'Because,' said Coco, 'We have to go back in the future, but we also need to drop you home safely, and we also have to make sure that you meet your mom, and, we need to save the apes as well.' He spoke.

'But why do *we* need to save them? A messiah is going to come to save them, right?' I asked. 'Yes, so we just go there and wait for him to come. Maybe, there is a chance that the messiah might have already come. We can't completely rely on the history, because we are still quite doubtful of the information provided.' Said the king.

'Oh.' I say although Coco had already told me about this. 'And, how much time is it going to take for us to reach?' I asked, 'Because I can't walk anymore.'

'According to me, it's not going to take over an hour to reach.' Said Coco. 'Yesterday,' I said, 'You told me that it was five hours away, and now you're telling me it's going to take another hour, I must say that your calculation is quite accurate.' I said sarcastically.

'You were the one who had the urge to touch a spiky-looking branch built in a death trap, and you even touched it, knowing that it could be dangerous! You just went like, ooh, looks like an interesting thing to eat, lets taste it. Oh no, its poison, we're all going to die, ah, run for your lives.' Said Coco mockingly.

'Hey, cool down guys, there's no need to fight.' Said the king. 'Coco,' he said, 'whatever you said wasn't required.' I smiled at him slyly and stuck out my tongue. 'And you, Aiden,' said the king, and I looked at him with that, "yes, I'm listening" expression, 'Why do you always need to do such stunts?' I looked at Coco who was sticking out his tongue and dancing hilariously as if saying *Who's the loser now, huh?*

'Shut it, Colson.' Said the king.

Coco grunted and crossed his arms. 'I will not tolerate such an attitude.' Said the king, facing Coco. I couldn't help smirking.

The king looked at me and I bit my lower lip to stop myself from smiling stupidly. I think the King noticed but didn't say anything even if he did.

As we walked for a few more minutes, the King suddenly stopped and looked down. 'Wait, don't move.' He said and stopped me by putting a hand in front of me. I stopped immediately. The first thoughts that came to my mind were, *oh God, where is the poison? Is it coming towards us? Oh! Is there a saber-toothed tiger somewhere?*

No, it's none of those, idiot. Said a voice in my head. 'Idiot!?' I said out loud. The king gave me a glance and raised an eyebrow. 'What did you just say, Aiden?' he asked, looking at me, and put his hands behind his back.

Coco looked at me and mouthed, *you're done, bro.*

'I wasn't saying it to you, I was saying it to my stick.' I said and smiled. The king didn't say anything but looked away.

I'm not a stick. Said an annoyed voice in my head. I couldn't help chuckling at the annoyed tone.

I was satisfied.

This time, Coco looked at me. This time, he was giving me a death stare.

'W-What's wrong?' I said, Coco's gaze making me shiver slightly. It was almost as if he could look into my soul.

The king, who was looking at the ground gave me a glance from the side of his eye, which made everything clear. 'So,' I asked, and looked forward, 'What are we looking at?'

'Gentlemen, I present to you the first kingdom of the apes ever formed.'

XXXIV
THE HUTS

I stared at a lake for a few seconds, searching for a kingdom built magnificently.

'Where's the kingdom?' I asked Coco. He looked at me and said, 'Oh, there is no kingdom. We built the first kingdom with a royal palace and all the luxurious stuff after the messiah saves the day.'

'Oh. But then where are the apes?' I asked. 'Uhm, can you see a cluster of a few huts on the other side of the lake?' he asked. I squinted my eyes and searched for the huts that Coco was pointing and when I finally spotted them, I nodded my head. 'Yeah, so they are the apes.' Said Coco.

'That's it?' I asked, astonished. 'Yeah, I know they are quite a few apes.' He spoke. 'How many are there approximately?' I asked. 'Not more than a hundred I guess.' Said Coco.

I was quite shocked by seeing how less the apes were. 'Are they losing?' I asked. That was a very stupid question, of course, they were losing. And dying. At a rapid speed. 'W-why? Whtuhat's happening?' I asked again.

'The robots are winning. As far as we know, it's not long before the messiah comes and saves us from going extinct.' Said Coco.

'Okay, and he or she is going to help us fix this watch as well, right?' I ask. 'No, the apes know how to fix this watch. The messiah doesn't. All we can do is request them to share the information with us. It's going to be a tough task to ask them for their help as they wouldn't be ready to give the information to us. They are very less in number, and they can't trust anyone. Not even their own kind. I mean, who will believe that we time-traveled and came here? The watch suddenly stopped working, and now, we need their help to fix this watch.' Said Coco.

'Yeah, you're right. Even I wouldn't believe you if I was in their place.' I spoke. 'But then, what does the king have in mind? What makes him so confident about our plan?' I asked. 'Do we even have a plan?' asked Coco. 'No, I said, but the king might have come up with something or the else.' I spoke.

'Shall we ask?' I asked. 'No, he'll tell us the plan himself.' Said Coco. 'If he has one.' Added Coco silently.

'Okay,' said the king and took a deep breath. 'Have you got any plans on how we can convince the apes to help us?' he asked.

Me and Coco shared a look and he said, 'I thought that you had already come up with a plan.'

'But,' I said, which made the king look at me, 'We cannot possibly know what the apes might ask us. Or maybe, they won't ask us and threaten to kill us the moment we appear. I mean, they are in a state of war, who has the time to sit and listen to what we say?' I asked.

'You're right, we cannot know what we are going to face there. So, we do everything on the spot. I do the speaking while you guys make sure that no one attacks.' Said the king.

'What if you are the first one to be captured?' asked Coco. 'Then, Aiden does the speaking.' Came the answer from the king almost immediately.

The king started to walk towards the huts in the distance.

'Bro, I'm so jealous of you right now.' Said Coco as we walked behind the king, maintaining a distance so the king couldn't overhear our conversation.

I chuckled, 'Why?' I asked. 'He likes you more than his son. And I'm not even adopted, or a stepson.' Said Coco.

'You never know Coco, always expect the unexpected.' I say jokingly. 'So, you think that I could be adopted?' asked Coco, his eyes widening in thought and surprise.

'No Coco, you are not adopted, nor do I like Aiden more than you. It's just that I think Aiden is more responsible than you.' Said the king from ahead.

I bit my tongue to stop myself from laughing out loud as I didn't want to hurt Coco's feelings because he looked quite serious when the king said that.

I knew that Coco was trying to prove himself to his dad, that he was responsible enough to handle things on his own. I had also known that the king had to give the throne to Coco in a few years, and he was just preparing Coco. I knew that the king loved and worried about Coco more than anyone, he was just too scared that his love would spoil Coco and he would not be worthy of the throne. He just loved Coco dearly, but he just didn't want to show it.

Now, how do I know all this? The king told me himself.

'Ok,' I say, 'now do we swim across this lake or do we just go around it?'

'We are going around it.' Said Coco.

Once we had crossed the lake, we started walking towards the huts. As we moved closer, some apes who were sharpening their axes turned to look at us. They kept staring at us for a few seconds before lifting up their axes threateningly.

The king noticed them and stopped immediately, and so did we. However, there was not the slightest sign of fear on his face.

Then, he made some sounds, which were in their language which I didn't understand.

'What is he saying?' I ask Coco. 'He is saying that we mean no harm and come in peace.' Said Coco. 'But then why can't he say the same thing in English? These apes know how to speak English, right?' I whisper. 'Yes, but even the robots know how to speak in English, but only the apes know how to speak in this language.' He said silently.

I nodded and then looked at the apes who were sharpening their axes. They lowered their weapons and looked at each other, wondering whether they could trust us or not.

Seeing their expressions, Coco said something in the same language and pointed at me. The apes seemed to trust us.

I was so glad that they didn't capture or try to kill us. At this point, I really needed the savior to come and get me out of this mess I had created for myself.

They called us in.

XXXV
THE CONDITION

The apes raised their weapon as we came closer. Seeing them, the other apes came from their huts and got ready to fight. They talked in their language and hopefully told the others that we meant no harm.

The other apes didn't look satisfied but didn't attempt to murder the moment we stood face to face. Although for me, it was leg-to-face, that's okay.

'Why are you here, and what do you want from us? You don't look like you're from around here.' said one elderly ape.

'You're right, we're not from here.' Said the king, 'We came from the future.' He spoke loudly. The elderly man laughed. 'Future, eh? Stop fooling around kid.' Said one of the apes from the back.

Seeing us, several more apes gathered around us, forming a big crowd. They leaned in to listen as the king mentioned the word 'future'.

'We are not fooling around, and this is no joke. We need your help. I know that you are building a time machine, and you know how to fix a broken one as well. I need you to fix this one.' Said the king and looked at me.

I raised my hand to show the watch.

There were a lot of gasps and then there was some whispering.

'Does anyone from outside know this? I doubt whether half of you know that they are building a time machine.' Said the king loudly.

'Is it true?' I heard an ape whisper.

The elderly ape raised a hand which silenced them all. The elderly ape faced the crowd and said, 'Yes, we are building a time machine, and we also know how to fix a broken one.' His voice was quite loud and strong for an ape of his age.

Hearing this, the king spoke, 'Then what are we waiting for, let's just get the work done and—'

'Not so soon,' interrupted the elderly man, which made the king frown slightly, 'everything comes with a price. If we are to help you, then you must help us in the war. If we win, then we will help you, but if we lose, then you'll have no one left to help you. Which we probably would. The robots have no mercy or emotions, no one will survive. I'm not discouraging anyone; I'm just telling you the truth which everyone knows but no one wants to accept.' He spoke sternly.

The king cleared his throat, which made everyone look at him, including the elderly ape. 'I have a better idea. You fix this watch as soon as possible and we bring our army from the future. We have quite a large army of around thousands. Now, what if we run away? We won't. I promise you that.' Said the king and made a series of complicated sounds which made the crowd gasp loudly, including Coco and the elderly man. The old ape's eyes widened in shock and surprise. It must've been a swear to someone very important to them.

Although the crowd looked in shock, the king sounded very confident in what he had said.

'What did he just say?' I asked Coco, whose mouth was open in awe and surprise. 'Y-you couldn't just have said that, father. I mean, if…' said Coco, still lost for words. 'Yes, my son, I just said that. I said exactly what you heard. The king smiled at him and patted his back.

Coco looked quite shocked by this sudden sign of affection from his father, but I could see that he liked it.

The elderly man allowed us to stay with them but made sure that an ape was keeping an eye on us all the time, just in case we tried to run away or do something.

In the evening, we were called for dinner. Although it was not quite grand, it tasted amazing.

Once we had finished eating, the elderly ape called us and took the watch from us to inspect it.

'Tomorrow,' he said, 'Come to that hut,' he pointed to one of the huts which was built a bit far from the rest of the village, 'after dinner, and you will find this watch fixed.' He spoke.

'Tomorrow!' exclaimed the king. 'Why, what's wrong with tomorrow?' he asked. 'Nothing's wrong with tomorrow. But, will you be able to repair it in a day? I mean that is impossible.' Said the king with curiosity.

The elderly man gave the king a *duh* expression that said, *if you don't believe it, then come tomorrow and check it yourself.*

XXXVI
THE WATCH IS FIXED

The next day, I woke up a bit early to the sounds of the birds and the forest.

The weather was quite pleasant and calm.

I yawned and stretched myself. I exercised a bit and jogged. I don't know why, but I had an urge to just get up and run around. I even made a friend, no, I made two friends. One was a squirrel and the other was a dog. The dog was domesticated by the apes. There were horse stables as well, and the horses were quite big (and by quite big, I mean very big). They were big enough to handle the weight of the apes. (I hope you remember that the apes are almost a hundred times my height.)

I was so busy playing with the dog that I didn't realize that it was lunchtime. Coco had called me for lunch.

After lunch, I went to play with the dog again. Time passed and it was dinnertime. I couldn't believe I didn't see the sun going down. The dog was the only animal that wasn't enlarged a hundred times its original size, or else I would have to ride it like an elephant.

I saw the commotion in the village and realized that it was dinnertime.

All the time during dinner, I was thinking about the watch.

After dinner, we patiently waited outside the hut the elderly ape had pointed to. I was about to knock on the door when it opened. The elderly ape looked at us and handed the watch to the king, and without saying anything, slammed the door shut in our faces.

Now that was quite rude.

We went to an open ground which was a bit away from the huts. I wanted to question why we couldn't do it a bit near the village, but I was way more excited to see the king time travel and bring the army.

'Stand back.' Said the king and we did as he said. We moved a few steps back. The king wore the watch and changed the time.

Then, there was a blinding light and there was a burnt outline of his footprints on the ground where he had stood.

We waited for a good ten minutes and then I asked Coco, 'Why hasn't he returned yet?'

'I guess we should not wait here any longer.' He said and then realized that I had spoken something before. He looked at me, puzzled. I repeated my question.

'Oh, see, when we came here, we arrived a bit later. A few years later in time. Thus, Father will mostly come back the next morning or at midnight. So, there's no point in waiting here.' He said in a matter-of-fact voice.

'Okay,' I say. 'Then the only thing I can think of doing right now is to sleep.'

Then, we both sleep.

XXXVII
GOSSIP!!!!

I was woken up again from my sleep, but this time, it was not by the birds chirping or the dog (Cooper) licking my face. I was woken up by a big light like someone had held a torch right above my eye.

I woke up, immediately realizing that the king had come with the army. I was so ready to see the reaction of the apes in the village after seeing an army of twenty thousand apes with such advanced weapons.

When I came out of my tent, I noticed that the apes were a lot more than last time, and, the sun had still not risen and the earth was still engulfed in darkness.

I approached the king and said, 'Good morning, Your Majesty. I remember that we did not have these many apes the last time I fought. How many are there?'

'Maybe a few million.' He spoke, as though a few million was not a big deal.

'WHAT!' I exclaimed, and then chuckled, 'T-that is quite a big army. But, last time, why did you say that we had an army of twenty thousand apes only? I asked.

'I wanted to see if you were worthy of being a messiah or not. I had these soldiers as a backup if things went completely out of hand. I wanted to see if you could manage to win when our army was almost five times smaller than the army of the robots. I knew you couldn't do it. But you proved me wrong.' He spoke and gave me a comforting smile.

I was not showered with so many compliments ever before, so I could think of nothing else to say except, 'Thank you.'

I wanted to say that it was all because of my killing machine and I was just a helping hand. But I didn't say it. Then, I realized that my stick was not there with me, but that was not of much importance. I mean, what will happen to it if I leave it alone for a few hours, it won't die, of course, and it has grown very annoying recently. Even if it gets broken in two halves, I won't shed a tear. I've developed a slight disliking to the way my stick talks to me.

Anyway, I can write a thousand page book describing vividly how annoying the Saber can be. So, lets get back to the story.

The army was making quite a lot of noise, which caused some apes to come out of their huts to see what was going on.

The sunrays pierced through the clouds and filled the earth with light.

As the morning sun slowly started to come up, the army became much clearer. A few apes gasped as they saw how big the army was.

I also spotted the elderly ape looking out from his window. At first, his eyes widened in surprise and then his mouth popped open. Then, his expression of surprise slowly turned into a scowl. I assume he was most probably thinking how he would feed such a gargantuan army.

Then I saw him draw the curtains and then opened the door to come out of the hut.

He cleared his throat loudly and said, 'Now, we mustn't waste any time and prepare for war. It's not long before the robots track us down. We'll also need to shift inside the forest as its easy to spot so many apes.'

Everyone nodded in agreement and looked at him, 'Why are you all staring at me? Go pack up your things!' he said, a hint of annoyance in his voice.

All of the apes, (the villagers. Wait, they weren't villagers exactly, they were just a bunch of common apes living there, together, to save themselves from the robots and from going extinct. So, every time I need to refer to these apes, I'll just write, "a bunch of common apes living there, together, to save themselves from the robots and from going extinct." uhm.... awkward silence...uh... You know what, I'll just stick to villagers.) scurried into their houses and within a few minutes, all of them were out of their huts with their belongings in their hands.

All this time, the elderly ape was just standing there, watching everyone pack their things and come out of their huts.

'Let's go then, what are we waiting for; AND STOP GIVING ME THOSE BLANK FACES!' he yelled.

Some apes just rolled their eyes, while the others looked at him with hatred and disgust, and the rest of them just looked done with their lives, they were just sitting there, staring at the old ape's face, and some people started whispering amongst themselves, most of them were girls. I wanted to go eavesdrop, but I resisted the urge to. I don't know exactly what they were saying but I know that they were talking trash about this old ape.

GOSSIP!!!!

[clears throat]

Sorry for going off track.

GOSSIP!!!

I was sure that the villagers had made a group of apes who disliked the old man.

Then, to express their pure hatred towards this ape, one of the kids shouted, 'Hey old FART!' (extra emphasis on "fart")

All of the villagers turned to look at that kid. Everybody cleared so that the elderly ape could get a clear view of him. He just stood there; his body stiffened. He gulped. Then, he ran into the forest as fast as he could. But unfortunately, he bumped into a tree and fainted. When we gathered around him to see if he was okay, he said that he could see stars in the sky. In the morning sun.

'Nah, he'll be fine.' I said with a flick of my hand.

XXXVIII
THE FOREST

He was not fine.

Anyways, I was right, the old fart - I mean the elderly ape was thinking about how he would be able to feed such a big army.

By the late afternoon, we were inside the forest, the hot noon sun was right above our heads, but, as we went deeper into the forest, it became denser and there were more spiky bushes. I was cautious not to come in contact with any spiky branches due to my past traumatic experience with spiky things. There was still a scar on my hand because of that.

Soon, there sunlight turned green. We were staying in the middle of the forest, where the animals and trees were the deadliest, and there were swamps. The sound of the wet mud below my shoes was making me really annoyed, and the same sound was made by the mud under the feet of the other apes.

Then, when we finalised a place to stay, my pant was completely soaked in mud and water was till my knees.

They started to build tents there and we decided to stay there for the rest of the night, or until the robots tracked our location.

It took them an hour to build all these, and I was of a huge help.

I was playing with Cooper.

I gave him some dog food and played with him. He kept wagging his tail. He was enjoying playing with me. I also spotted some apes staring at me, talking about me. Most probably admiring how useless I was. I was really proud of my quality of uselessness.

I smiled at them but they only scowled. I tell you, the kids these days...

While I was working very hard to help build the tents, the king came to me and said, 'Hey,' I looked up, 'What are you doing?'

I gesture towards the dog. When you can see what I'm doing, why do you need to ask 'I'm eating fruits.' I say, 'do you want some?' I ask sarcastically.

The king sighs, finally realizing my uselessness. Maybe, I'll publish a book named, "the power of uselessness-by Aiden Anderson."

Sorry, going off-track again.

'Aiden,' he said, 'a word?'

I get up and follow him. Once we were at a good distance from the villagers, he said, 'The robots will track us down any moment now. When is the messiah coming?'

'How should I know?' I ask.

The king thinks for some time and says, 'I think that no messiah is going to come.' He said, looking at my confused expression, he said, 'The messiah had already arrived.'

I burst with joy and jumped around. 'Oh my god! Where is he?' I start looking between the trees. Hoping to find someone who looks brave, muscularly built, with determination in his eyes.

I notice the king looking at me and I realize what he's trying to say.

'Seriously? Me. Again?'

XXXIX
THE SHOUT

Okay, so now, I have to save the world again. Yay! So fun, let's almost die again!

So, I hadn't even agreed to whether I wanted to save the world again, I had no option. I didn't want to lead such a big army again, it was quite a big headache, but, what other option did I have? Quitting? Somebody would kill me before I quitted, so...nope.

The king told everyone that I was going to help them, and I was their messiah. The whole army was very happy, but the villagers still thought that I was a hopeless case, and they looked very unhappy about the king's decision.

'I'm sorry to interrupt, but we can't give our lives in the hand of a kid.' Said the elderly man. I was quite annoyed that he called me a kid, but I took a few deep breaths to calm myself down.

'How can we depend on this good-for-nothing boy to save our lives?' the elderly ape pointed to me. Every villager seemed to agree.

When he called me good-for-nothing, I was now biting my tongue to prevent myself from saying something rude, but I was still a bit annoyed. 'Good-for-nothing, you say, huh? Okay then, you are on your own. We're not going to help you. I have my watch. I can go back anytime. The king knows what he's doing.' I tried to convince them that I could save them, my voice was cracking up from controlling my anger for so long.

'How can we trust you?' asked one of the apes from the crowd.

I couldn't think of a proper answer. I couldn't say anything, I didn't have any plans on how I could kill the robots. I had no rights to give them fake hopes. But I had won once and I could do it again.

'Okay then,' said the old man after a few seconds of thinking, 'I trust you, but don't let us down.'

'I won't. I promise.' I said, grateful that he finally trusted me.

I looked at the king and saw him widen his eyes as he looked at the old ape. 'Uhm... mister,' said the king with so much respect that I almost choked on my saliva.

The old man looked at the king, 'By any chance, do you have a son?' asked the king. The old ape nodded. The king looked at me and said that clearly said that we needed to talk.

The king took me aside and said, 'He's the father of the ape who found this watch.' He said, very excited. 'Remember to treat him with respect. It is because of him that we can time travel.'

I cleared my throat, 'Correction, his son made the watch, by which we can time travel now, so I will treat his son with respect. How is he involved with all this respect thing?'

The king glared at me, 'That's what, *his* son made the watch, that's why we should respect *him*. Without *him*, his son would never have been born.'

'So,' I said, 'then, we should treat this old ape's ancestors respectfully as well, because he descended from them, which could be a fish as well.'

The king folded his arms. 'You will treat him respectfully, is that clear, Aiden?'

His tone clearly said that I had no other option, and if I said no, I would get stamped like an ant under his foot, or get slapped by him which would end up dislocating all the bones in my body.

I nodded.

'Good.' Said the king and smiled warmly at me. I smiled back at him.

Before the king could say anything else, we heard a loud shriek of an ape. It alerted everyone. I looked alarmingly at her. We all rushed towards her to ask what she shouted for.

She looked frozen. She was drenched in cold sweat. She was frozen in shock. Everyone had gathered around her, which made her even more afraid to speak.

'Move,' I said, but the whisperings and the murmurings were so loud that my voice was hardly audible. I took a few steps back and shouted, 'MOVE!'

They all looked at me and a few jumped in surprise. The look on my face must've been quite serious, so they moved. I looked at the ape who had shouted. 'Miss, what happened?' I asked softly, trying to comfort her, which was quite hard for me as she was so big. I looked like an ant.

The ape looked at me. She looked at me right in the eye, and something inside me told to keep my eyes locked with hers. Then, she broke the eye contact.

'T-they,' she began, her voice breaking with fear and worry. 'They what?' I asked, trying not to sound too eager.

'T-they t-took him.' She spoke, then she broke into soft silent sobs and buried her face in her hands. I knew I didn't have to ask twice.

Then, from the crowd emerged Coco, and he said, 'Miss, who is the person you are talking about? It must've been a silly prank, or it was just his friends. You don't have to worry so much.' And put a hand on her shoulder.

Coco looked at me. I looked right into his eyes. Then, his gaze drifted to my clenched fists. He widened his eyes ever so slightly and looked at me. I was looking at the ground when he looked back at me. I gulped and looked into his eyes. He widened his eyes even more.

I walked through the crowd, away from the ape who was sobbing. I was aware that Coco was looking at me as I walked away.

XL
THE FIRST ATTACK

We both knew what was coming, and so did the king, and I was glad I didn't have to explain it all to him.

I went and stood on a raised platform so that I could be visible to all. I wasn't sure if anyone was going to believe it.

But I had to try.

I cleared my throat as loud as possible, as I could think of no other way to catch everyone's attention. All the apes looked at me, their attention was on me but that only increased the murmurings of the crowd.

Edward, the commanding officer looked at me with his spear ready in his arms. With a nod of my head, I permitted him. Then, he went to the king. They talked silently for a few seconds and Edward bowed his head down and walked away.

'We're under attack.' I said loudly, 'The robots have tracked down our location, and it's the robots that have taken the ape. It's not long before they start attacking us.' I said, and everyone seemed to understand the urgency in my voice.

I didn't know what else to say, so, I got down and went near the king.

'Uhm, what should we do now? We don't have any weapons for the villagers. We can't leave them defenceless, right?' I asked the king.

'We do have extra weapons, although, I'm not sure how many are there.' He replied, his voice a bit sterner than usual. 'Edward should know how many are there.' He spoke. I nodded.

I ran towards Edward, and by the time I reached him, I was panting. 'We need extra weapons. For the villagers.' I said with my hands on my knees, panting.

Edward and I walked for a few seconds before he pointed behind a tree. 'The weapons are kept behind the tree.' He spoke. I took a look at the weapons. They were enough to provide weapons to at least half the villagers. The weapons were shields and spears, classic. However, I had imagined that people in the future must have some very advanced tech which was quite hard to understand.

The weapons were quite big for me. I needed my stick. I then realized that I had forgotten it somewhere. I closed my eyes and summoned the wooden stick. Then, I heard a hum near my ear. I opened my eyes to find a stick levitating beside me.

Hey. I thought. *I need help in carrying these weapons.* I was waiting for it to reply sarcastically.

Then, the stick glowed golden and an invisible force lifted the weapons. I was quite surprised that it didn't argue or talk back. It had understood the urgency of the situation. There was no time to waste. I gripped the staff and levitated a few millimetres above the ground.

We reached the place where the villagers were gathered together. They saw me coming with weapons.

I dropped the weapons on the ground and the apes looked at the weapons. 'Everyone will be using these weapons to fight alongside us. It is not safe for you to stay here, defenceless. There are chances that you might get captured or killed by the robots while we're fighting, and we won't even get to know. So, we have decided that you will be fighting alongside us.' I said loudly.

The staff handed a spear and a shield to each one of the apes. 'We don't have time, and we don't know when they will be attacking. It might be the very next second.' I said at the top of my voice. I hesitated for a second before saying this. 'Look at your loved ones one last time, because you don't know whether you'll ever see them again. If you fought with them, don't let it be the last memory you have of them.' I didn't want that to happen. My mom was sick, and I don't even know whether her health worsened or did it become better because I had no expectations from Logan.

Just then, something hit my head and fell on the ground. 'Ow!' I complained and rubbed the back of my head. I looked at the ground to see what had hit me. It looked like a thermometer but in the shape of an arrow. It had a digital reading on it. I looked at the digital reading after pulling the arrow out of the ground.

It had a countdown, with five minutes left. At first, I couldn't understand what it was, but then, the realization hit me with a shock. My whole body went cold and numb when I realized what it was. My mouth became dry. It was as if I had sand in my mouth. I didn't know how to tell them. Time was ticking. Even if I threw it, I couldn't save everyone, if we ran away, apes would still die, I couldn't break it, I couldn't fly away with it. I gulped. I broke out in cold sweat as I realize the destruction it could cause. I took a deep breath, trying to calm myself down, but you guys are very well aware of how good I am at calming myself down. This was not a big deal, but I was panicking, which did not help things get better.

Now, what was this thing that made my legs wobbly?

It was a time bomb.

XLI

GET READY TO FIGHT!

'RUN!' I screamed at the top of my lungs and asked my wooden stick to take this as far as possible. I screamed run as I didn't know what the range of this bomb was and also; to be on the safer side.

Panic was created at my sudden shout, as expected. There was screaming and apes, especially the villagers, were running in all directions, which was creating a mess. 'Everyone, please stop running around.' I spoke loudly, but no one was listening to me. I tried again. No luck.

I cleared my throat once more. 'STOP SCREAMING AND RUNNING AROUND LIKE A BUNCH OF TOTAL MORONS!' I screamed at the top of my lungs, which, thankfully, caught the attention of most of the apes. I smiled at all of them, but there was a hint of irritation in it, 'Stop panicking guys. If you keep running around like this, someone is ought to get left behind, so stick together.' I said sweetly, or at least I tried to.

'Military, stay with them for their security and move away as far as possible, but keep an eye out for the robots.' I said and looked at Edward. The villagers jogged with the army and started to move away, however, Coco and the king stayed with me.

Then, a familiar voice spoke in my head, *I'm returning and I've thrown the bomb as far as I could. I am not able to study the weapon, so I can't give you much information about it. But I can tell you that it is a new type of atomic bomb. An atomic bomb that will cause way more destruction than you could ever imagine.*

I clear my throat, 'How are you telling me this, where are you?' I ask, not too loudly, so that people don't think I'm mad.

Our minds are now connected, dumbo. So, no matter how far you are from me, I can still communicate with you. Said the voice of the stick in my head.

Okay, I thought, trying not to sound too irritated by it calling me a dumbo, but I had forgotten that it could read my emotions as well, *how much time will you take to come back here?*

There was no reply, but something hit me on the back of my head. I turned around and found my magical wooden stick levitating a few centimeters above the ground.

I was so glad to find that it wasn't an atomic bomb. 'How far did you take it?' I asked it.

Ten thousand eighty hundred nineteen kilometers away. Said its voice in my head.

Good, I think, *then we're safe.*

Just then, a strong wind blew, and fine sand particles went into my eyes, which made them sting. I closed my eyes shut. The sudden wind was so strong that it knocked me off my feet and I fell on the ground. I heard the sound of wind gushing in my ears, and blood roared in them. The wind was hitting my face like needles. After a few thirty seconds, the wind stopped and everything came back to normal, as if nothing had happened. I opened my eyes and looked around to see that several trees had been uprooted.

I took time to find my voice, and once I did, I shouted, 'What in the world was *that*?!'

It was a shock wave caused by the atomic bomb. Said the voice in my head immediately. *Imagine the destruction it could've caused if we didn't move it away on time.*

I shivered just thinking of it. A trail of goosebumps erupted on my skin. With that very beautiful thought, I got up and blinked my eyes a few times to get the sand out of my eyes.

I took the levitating staff in my hand and it suddenly glowed. The stick flew from my hand and levitated a meter away from my head. Then, its voice said in my head, *Duck.*

Duck? I thought, and I looked around but didn't find a group of ducks anywhere around. I then looked up at the sky to see hundreds of arrows coming towards us.

I covered my head and ducked. Only out of curiosity, I looked up and saw that the staff was spinning above my head and was preventing any arrows from falling on me. The arrows were endless, they just kept coming. They came for at least a minute before they stopped.

Thank you, was all I could think at that point. *I don't know what I would've done without you.* I thought.

We should leave, the rest of the apes are far ahead of us. Said the voice in my head. I agreed to it, and we flew till the time we spotted the group of apes and I landed right in front of them, and I was shocked that I landed so smoothly.

'So now,' I began loudly. 'We move towards their base and attack them when they haven't noticed that we're there so that we can kill at least one-fourth of the robots. But we have to make sure that we do it as quickly and silently as possible.' Everybody seemed to understand that. 'Is this clear?' I asked them, although there was nothing so complicated about it. They all nodded their heads.

'Okay, so how many of us are there?' I asked. 'Two million.' Said the king. I tried not to sound too surprised by the number. 'Okay, two million, and the villagers?' I asked. 'I guess a few fifty. Most of them are children.' Said the elderly ape.

I nodded my head and said, 'Okay, now our priority is to keep the children safe. I want fifty of our men to stay with the children.' I spoke. But then the king said, 'No Aiden, according to me, it's better to keep all the villagers together. Let's not make them fight the war with us, it'll be a burden for us while fighting. We can't risk the safety of the villagers just for the sake of winning.' He said quietly so that only I could hear what he said. I nodded my head in understanding, 'I am changing my decision, I want one-hundred fifty of our soldiers to protect the villagers, you will not be fighting with us.' I turned towards the villagers while speaking.

The first line of the soldiers came and gathered around the group of villagers. Edward ordered the soldiers to go back inside the forest and to keep the villagers hidden from the eyes of the robot.

We kept walking, as silently as possible, although we could fly with the help of my staff, we preferred not to take any risks. We followed Coco's lead as he claimed to know where the robots' stronghold was.

While walking, Coco suddenly stopped and so did we, suddenly getting more alert than before. I knew we were walking into the jaws of death if we were caught. I had no idea how many of them were out there. But it couldn't be more than what I had seen during the last battle I had fought. Could it?

There were thick bushes that were blocking our view. I made a gesture with my hand that said *take your position.*

They took all their positions. The first three rows were of the archers, they were ready to shoot their arrows as soon as they got a clear view. But getting a clear view of the enemy could probably give away our positions as well.

But I didn't care about that. Before they could detect our presence, we would shoot them down. Then, I remembered something. I made a gesture with my hands that said *hold.* The archers looked at me.

'Just saying,' I began, 'you have to aim for the center of the chest of the robot, where the chip is stored. If you destroy it, there's no chance of it regenerating.'

Everybody took their aims and released the arrows. The moment they did so, I got ready with my stick. I took my position, standing in front of the army, ready for anything.

XLII

THE FORCE FIELD

I heard the arrows cut through the air and land on their targets. I subconsciously gripped my weapon tighter. Small beads of sweat formed on my forehead, and then slowly began to trickle down my face, showing how nervous I was.

My weapon started to glow, and for some reason, I knew exactly what to do. I raised the wooden stick high above my head and brought it down to the earth with all my force, channelizing all my strength to my hand. As the stick hit the ground, the impact made the whole ground shake.

At first, the force field appeared as a translucent dome with hues of blue and golden energy sparkling throughout as the dome was getting formed. There was a very slight sound of energy crackling in the air.

When the dome had covered the whole army, it sent another vibration which almost knocked me out of my feet.

I looked up and found several arrows coming back at us. Then, I realized that they were the arrows that we had shot. None of the robots were dead.

I gripped the staff tighter and held it with both my hands. I knew that the stick was going to get damaged, and I was not going to have it with me for half the battle.

'How much damage is it going to cause you?' I asked.

I won't be there with you with half the battle. It spoke in my head.

'Knew it.' I muttered under my breath. I was halfway hoping it would say that it wouldn't cause him any damage.

If you already knew it, then why did you ask? It spoke.

The arrows hit the force field. The light of the stick wavered and the force field broke. I suddenly felt shooting pain in my entire body. My arms and legs felt like jelly. They had gone numb. I couldn't feel them, nor could I control them. My grip on the staff was loosening.

I couldn't fall on the ground and scare everyone. We couldn't lose this. I couldn't break my promise. I tried to take hold of the staff again, but my fingers weren't listening to me.

Then, I experienced something that had never happened to me before, and this wasn't the best place to experience that. I tried to keep calm. I didn't know what to do. Basically, I was paralyzed. Not for lifetime, only for a limited time. But that was a nightmare. I got paralyzed, in between of a battle. I hadn't fainted, but I felt all the energy drain out of my body as I slowly let go of the staff and started to fall on the ground. Something had happened to me as I fell.

I blacked out.

When the suspense was building.

I hate my life.

XLIII
THE F13A SABER

When I woke up, I found several apes around me. Maybe two or three. I saw that my staff was on the ground. I tried to pick it up, but I couldn't feel my fingers, they were still numb. I brought my hands and rubbed them together to create some blood circulation. After a few seconds, I felt blood rush to my fingers. I felt relieved as I felt my fingers again.

As I got up, I felt blood rush to my legs. I picked up my staff that was on the ground, yet, it wasn't glowing.

'Hey buddy, you there?' I asked softly.

There was no reply. The staff was still not fully powered, and there was no way that I could fight the war without him. I was a helpless little ant without it. It was then, when I realized that all the weapons were powered by the staff.

I looked from between two trees, the apes were fighting, some of them had died, which was very painful. It was a war, and no war could be won without blood. So, I tried to make myself understand that this was ok.

But I felt bad that I wasn't able to help them in any ways as my stick was powered down. But I needed to be a part of the war. I would die the moment I entered the battlefield.

'Do we still have the backup weapons?' I asked the soldiers. After a few minutes of waiting, the soldiers brought a shield and a spear which was five times my size. I was going to ask them how I was supposed to fight with such enormous weapons when they pressed something on the shield and spear which shrunk them in size. 'Thanks.' I said when the handed me the weapons. I was just going to leave when I asked them, 'Aren't you guys coming?'

'No, his majesty has asked us to keep an eye on the F13A Saber, so that the robots aren't able to break it, because this can be broken with ease when not powered.' Said one of the robots. I nodded as I heard them.

'Please be careful.' I say, concerned, although the Saber had been insulting me very much lately. It was the only source of power I had with me, and I didn't want to lose it.

I went through the trees and entered the battleground. The moment I entered; I narrowly missed a laser beam shot at me. I took a deep breath and activated the shield. It immediately formed a force field around me, protecting me from all the attacks. I spotted an ape who was struggling to fight with a group of robots. His arm was twisted in a weird angle, and he was only fighting with one arm. I made my way through the giants and jumped on one of the robots. Before it could detect me, I hit the chip and the robot evaporated on the spot.

The ape looked at me, gratefully. I smiled very slightly at him, a curve tugging at my lips. As one of his arms was twisted, he could either hold the spear, or the shield, and he decided to fight as he had no other choice because his shield was broken in two halves.
I continued fighting the robots, and I had an advantage as I could move around faster that the robot because of my size. After evaporating one of the robots to dust, I remembered that the king had told me that the weapons were made from the strongest metal on the planet, which was almost unbreakable. The shield of the ape was broken in two halves, indicating just how powerful the robots were. I realized that these robots were stronger than the ones I had fought with previously.

With that thought, I started to look around to see if I found Coco or the king anywhere. But there were no signs of either of them.

While fighting, I noticed that the shield and the spear had similar markings to that of the F13A Saber. The markings were also etched on the on the weapon, which was glowing a dim yellow. I realized that when I made the force field to protect the apes, the spear and shield was glowing golden, as bright as my wooden stick. Now, instead of the light increasing, the light was getting dimmer by the minute, which made me a bit worried. If the power of the staff was not returning, then we would have a hard time fighting the robots. Either we die fighting, or we surrender, and I was not going to surrender, no way.

So, I decided to go check on my wooden stick. Not because I was worried about it, but because I didn't want to lose the battle, not after so much hope I gave the apes. If they got to know that the power of the staff was dying out, they will break down, and if our army is not mentally strong, we won't be able to fight. On top of that, even our army from the future was here, so if we all die, we'll have no army in the future. If the robots are still alive, (which is not possible) they would have no one to stop them from taking control over the earth (in the future i.e. where I first met Coco).

I dodged the laser beams and narrowly missed a spear coming at me. I was just about to reach the trees behind which my staff was kept and the guards were protecting it, when a robot blocked my way by shooting a laser beam at me. Subconsciously, I put my shield in front of me to prevent myself from getting hit.

The laser beam made a hole right beside my head. Maybe an inch away, so even if I moved a bit or the placing of my head was a centimetre different, the laser would have shot me right in the eye.

But when the laser hit the shield, small cracks started to form from the hole and started to spread across the whole shield until pieces of it fell from my hand until the whole thing collapsed at my foot.

I was too stunned to speak for a while until the robot shot another laser beam at me, which I could dodge but a few strands of my hair could not, and they burnt to ashes. I took a bit jump, yet I could only reach its leg, I climbed up with the help of the spear, dodging all attacks. One of its laser beams brushed against my cheek and passed by, forming a clean cut through which blood began to flow.

Despite the pain, I continued climbing it until I hit the chip and it evaporated into ashes. As I regained my balance after falling to the ground, I started to make my way towards the bushes when I suddenly felt all the power drain from me, and blood roared in my ears. For only a mere second, the shield felt heavy in my arms. Only for a mere second, I felt weak. I was now certain that there was something very wrong.

I went towards the place behind the trees where my stick was kept. There were no guards around it. There were no guards to protect it, and then, I felt that the weapons in my hands weighed a ton. So, to prevent my hands from falling off, I threw the weapons on the ground.

When I looked at the stick in front of my eyes, I was speechless. I was dumbfounded.

There it was, the F13A Saber, on the ground, powerless.

Broken in two halves.

XLIV
THE END

I went on my knees to scoop it up in my arms. My vision started to turn blurry. My eyes were watering. As I blinked, a tear fell on the ground.

'A-are you there, buddy?' I asked, my voice choked with emotion.

Yes, I am there, boss. Said a weak voice in my head, and the Saber glowed a dim yellow.

Don't start crying like a baby. We both know if I was a person, I would just roll my eyes at you. It spoke in my head as I gave a sad chuckle. For some reason, my heart ached to see the stick in this way. I tightened my grip on the staff.

I may not return, but you're never alone. Honor our bond, and I'll be with you in spirit. It paused for a moment before speaking again. *You'll be fine without me, boss. Just try not to accidentally stab yourself. Although I won't be there by your side anymore, I expect you to stay alive, and if you dare die, I will haunt you.* It said, trying to lighten the mood.

'Shut up.' I said, feeling annoyed and emotional at the same time. I was annoyed at the fact that it was trying to make me smile. It only chuckled at my annoyed yet emotional tone. I totally forgot that it could read my mind as well.

So, I guess this is our goodbye, boss. It said sadly. 'Don't you dare say that.' I said softly. *Don't try to convince yourself that I won't die. It* spoke in my head. I held on to it tightly. 'Please don't go.' I muttered to it.

Meet you on the other side. Goodbye, kiddo. It spoke.

I smiled with pain at the nickname it gave me. 'Goodbye, stick.' I whispered. I hugged it tightly. I closed my eyes as I cried silently. I sat there for a few minutes looking at the staff, my insides burning with anger and several other jumbled emotions.

I stood up and carefully placed the wooden staff on the ground. I tried to lift my weapons again, but they were too heavy, just like the burden on my heart. I felt that *I* was the one responsible for the death of the staff. I felt guilty.

As I wasn't able to lift the weapons, I decided to go into the battle, unarmed. I couldn't leave the others alone. My head was still throbbing as I had cried and my eyes were still puffy.

As I entered the battlefield once more, I wanted to kill myself on the spot.

All the apes had dropped their weapons and they were on their knees. Their hands were above their heads and there was a spear pointed at their necks. As I took in the scene, I heard a robotic voice.

'Aha! There you are, Aiden.' Said the robot and walked towards me. My blood was boiling after seeing the dead staff and I felt like punching the robot right in the face but I knew it would only make matters worse. I wanted to go shout in front of the apes to fight, but not give up.

As though the robot read my mind, it came closer and whispered in my ear. 'There's no point fighting a lost battle.'

I got goosebumps at the sound of it. I clenched my fists, trying to control my anger and annoyance.

'So, the F13A Saber is destroyed.' It said, and I felt my eyes water again. I wiped my tears and tried not to break down in front of my whole army.

'There's no point fighting this, Aiden. You and your little army will die in a blink. We have overpowered you. You are nothing in front of us.' It said loudly.

All the apes looked at the robot with hatred in their eyes. My fists had turned white and I was now taking deep breaths to keep my cool. 'Kill them.' said the robot and looked at me. I looked up at the robots and shouted at the top of my lungs, 'NO!'

'Don't kill them.' Said the robot calmly, and I breathed a sigh of relief. 'We will kill them.' It spoke. 'Decide one, kill them, or don't.' I said, annoyed. 'First you say you will kill them, then you say you don't, and now again you want to kill them. Can't you make up your mind about something?' I asked them, a hint of impatience and anger in my voice.

Completely ignoring me, the robot continued, 'You want to save them, huh?' it asked me. Of course I wanted to save the apes, what kind of question was that?!

'Yes.' I spoke. 'That is what I expected from you, Aiden. Ok, so now, you have two choices, either you trade their lives for yours, or... yours for them.' It said in a deeper, and more devilish tone.

Without thinking even for a second, I put my hands above my head and put one knee on the ground. 'I surrender. Let them go.' I said with closed eyes.

There were several gasps from the apes, and I couldn't blame them. I was trading my life for theirs.

'Very well then.' Said the robots as they picked me up from my collar. 'But you are not even allowed to touch the apes.' I spoke. 'Yeah, yeah, we won't harm them.' Said the robot. 'Let them go.' It spoke

So, I guess this is how it ends.

I surrender.

I trade my life for theirs, and I have no regrets.